WINNING SEASON

The college widow goes down in a plane crash...the coach is reduced to a wheelchair...the team's only black star gives up football to study mysticism...the runningback gives up mysticism to study nuclear war...and meanwhile the coaches chant: "Hit somebody, hit somebody...."

END ZONE

"BRILLIANT"—*Baltimore Sun*

"The book is powerfully funny...tearing along in dazzling cinematic spurts...twisting and bobbing like Groucho Marx on a faked end run...."—*Book World*

"FOOTBALL FANTASIES THAT WOULD MAKE EVEN ALEX KARRAS ENVIOUS...."
—*The New York Times*

S0-ADK-474

END ZONE
was originally published by
Houghton Mifflin Company.

Also by Don DeLillo

Americana

 Are there paperbound books you want but cannot find in your retail stores?

Don DeLillo

END ZONE

PUBLISHED BY POCKET BOOKS NEW YORK

END ZONE

Houghton Mifflin edition published March, 1972

POCKET BOOK edition published April, 1973

Portions of this book originally appeared in **The New Yorker**
and **Works in Progress.**

This POCKET BOOK edition includes every word
contained in the original, higher-priced edition. It is printed
from brand-new plates made from completely reset, clear, easy-to-read
type. POCKET BOOK editions are published by POCKET BOOKS, a division
of Simon & Schuster, Inc., 630 Fifth Avenue, New York, N.Y. 10020.
Trademarks registered in the United States and other countries.

Standard Book Number: 671-78282-7.
Library of Congress Catalog Card Number: 77-177544.
This POCKET BOOK edition is published by arrangement with
Houghton Mifflin Company.

Printed in the U.S.A.   Cover photograph by Shig Ikeda.

To my parents

Part One

1

TAFT ROBINSON WAS the first black student to be enrolled at Logos College in west Texas. They got him for his speed.

By the end of that first season he was easily one of the best running backs in the history of the Southwest. In time he might have turned up on television screens across the land, endorsing eight-thousand-dollar automobiles or avocado-flavored instant shave. His name on a chain of fast-food outlets. His life story on the back of cereal boxes. A drowsy monograph might be written on just that subject, the modern athlete as commercial myth, with footnotes. But this doesn't happen to be it. There were other intonations to that year, for me at least, the phenomenon of anti-applause—words broken into brute sound, a consequent silence of metallic texture. And so Taft Robinson, rightly or wrongly, no more than haunts this book. I think it's fitting in a way. The mansion has long been haunted (double metaphor coming up) by the invisible man.

But let's keep things simple. Football players are simple folk. Whatever complexities, whatever dark politics of the human mind, the heart—these are noted only within the chalked borders of the playing field. At times strange visions ripple across that turf; madness leaks out. But wherever else he goes, the football player travels the straightest of lines. His thoughts are wholesomely commonplace, his actions uncomplicated by history, enigma, holocaust or dream.

A passion for simplicity, for the true old things, as of boys on bicycles delivering newspapers, filled our days and nights that fierce summer. We practiced in the undulating heat with nothing to sustain us but the conviction that things here were simple. Hit and get hit: key the pulling guard; run over people; suck some ice and reassume the three-point stance. We were a lean and dedicated squad run by a hungry coach and his seven oppressive assistants. Some of us were more simple than others; a few might be called outcasts or exiles; three or four, as on every football team, were crazy. But we were all—even myself—we were all dedicated.

We did grass drills at a hundred and six in the sun. We attacked the blocking sleds and strutted through the intersecting ropes. We stood in what was called the chute (a narrow strip of ground bordered on two sides by blocking dummies) and we went one on one, blocker and pass-rusher, and hand-fought each other to the earth. We butted, clawed and kicked. There were any number of fistfights. There was one sprawling free-for-all, which the coaches allowed to continue for about five minutes, standing on the sidelines looking pleasantly bored as we kicked each other in the shins and threw dumb rights and lefts at caged faces, the more impulsive taking off their helmets and swinging them at anything that moved. In the evenings we prayed.

I was one of the exiles. There were many times, believe it, when I wondered what I was doing in that remote and unfed place, that summer tundra, being hit high and low by a foaming pair of 240-pound Texans. Being so tired and sore at night that I could not raise an arm to brush my teeth. Being made to obey the savage commands of unreasonable men. Being set apart from all styles of civilization as I had known or studied them. Being led in prayer every evening, with the rest of the squad, by our coach, warlock and avenging patriarch. Being made to lead a simple life.

Then they told us that Taft Robinson was coming to

school. I looked forward to his arrival—an event, finally, in a time of incidents and small despairs. But my teammates seemed sullen at the news. It was a break with simplicity, the haunted corner of a dream, some piece of forest magic to scare them in the night.

Taft was a transfer student from Columbia. The word on him was good all the way. (1) He ran the hundred in 9.3 seconds. (2) He had good moves and good hands. (3) He was strong and rarely fumbled. (4) He broke tackles like a man pushing through a turnstile. (5) He could pass-block—when in the mood.

But mostly he could fly—a 9.3 clocking for the hundred. Speed. He had sprinter's speed. Speed is the last excitement left, the one thing we haven't used up, still naked in its potential, the mysterious black gift that thrills the millions.

2

(EXILE OR OUTCAST: distinctions tend to vanish when the temperature exceeds one hundred.)

Taft Robinson showed up at the beginning of September, about two weeks before regular classes were to start. The squad, originally one hundred bodies, soon down to sixty, soon less, had reported in the middle of August. Taft had missed spring practice and twenty days of the current session. I didn't think he'd be able to catch up. I was in the president's office the day he arrived. The president was Mrs. Tom Wade, the founder's widow. Everybody called her Mrs. Tom. She was the only woman I had ever seen who might accurately be described as Lincolnesque. Beyond appearance I had no firm idea of her reality; she was tall, black-browed, stark as a railroad spike.

I was there because I was a northerner. Apparently they thought my presence would help make Taft feel at home, an idea I tended to regard as laughable. (He was from Brooklyn, having gone on to Columbia from Boys High, a school known for the athletes it turns out.) Mrs. Tom and I sat waiting.

"My husband loved this place," she said. "He built it out of nothing. He had an idea and he followed it through to the end. He believed in reason. He was a man of reason. He cherished the very word. Unfortunately he was mute."

"I didn't know that."

"All he could do was grunt. He made disgusting sounds. Spit used to collect at both corners of his mouth. It wasn't a real pretty sight."

Taft walked in flanked by our head coach, Emmett Creed, and backfield coach, Oscar Veech. Right away I estimated height and weight, about six-two, about 210. Good shoulders, narrow waist, acceptable neck. Prize beef at the county fair. He wore a dark gray suit that may have been as old as he was.

Mrs. Tom made her speech.

"Young man, I have always admired the endurance of your people. You've a tough row to hoe. Frankly I was against this from the start. When they told me their plan, I said it was bushwah. Complete bushwah. But Emmett Creed is a mighty persuasive man. This won't be easy for any of us. But what's reason for if not to get us through the hard times? There now. I've had my say. Now you go on ahead with Coach Creed and when you're all thoo talking football you be sure to come on back here and see Mrs. Berry Trout next door. She'll get you all settled on courses and accommodations and things. History will be our ultimate judge."

Then it was my turn.

"Gary Harkness," I said. "We're more or less neighbors. I'm from upstate New York."

"How far up?" he said.

"Pretty far. Very far in fact. Small town in the Adirondacks."

We went over to the players' dorm, an isolated unit just about completed but with no landscaping out front and WET PAINT signs everywhere. I left the three of them in Taft's room and went downstairs to get suited up for afternoon practice. Moody Kimbrough, our right tackle and captain on offense, stopped me as I was going through the isometrics area.

"Is he here?"

"He is here," I said.

"That's nice. That's real nice."

In the training room Jerry Fallon had his leg in the whirlpool. He was doing a crossword puzzle in the local newspaper.

"Is he here?"

"He is everywhere," I said.

"Who?"

"Supreme being of heaven and earth. Three letters."

"You know who I mean."

"He's here all right. He's all here. Two hundred and fifty-five pounds of solid mahogany."

"How much?" Fallon said.

"They're thinking of playing him at guard. He came in a little heavier than they expected. About two fifty-five. Left guard, I think Coach said."

"You kidding me, Gary?"

"Left guard's your spot, isn't it? I just realized."

"How much is he weigh again?"

"He came in at two fifty-five, two sixty. Solid bronze right from the foundry. Coach calls him the fastest two-five-five in the country."

"He's supposed to be a running back," Fallon said.

"That was before he added the weight."

"I think you're kidding me, Gary."

"That's right," I said.

"You son of a bitch," Fallon said.

We ran through some new plays for about an hour. Creed's assistants moved among us yelling at our mistakes. Creed himself was up in the tower studying overall patterns. I saw Taft on the sidelines with Oscar Veech. The players kept glancing that way. When the second unit took over on offense, I went over to the far end of the field and grubbed around for a spot of shade in which to sit. Finally I just sank into the canvas fence and remained more or less upright, contemplating the distant fury. These canvas blinds surrounded the entire practice field in order to discourage spying by future opponents. The blinds were one of the many innovations Creed had come up with—innovations as far as this particular college was concerned. He had also had the tower built as well as the separate living quarters for the football team. (To instill a sense of unity.) This was Creed's first year here. He had been born in Texas, in either a log cabin or a manger, depending on who was telling the story, on the banks of the Rio Grande in what is now Big Bend National Park. The sporting press liked to call him Big Bend. He made a few all-American teams as a tailback in the old single-wing days at SMU and then flew a B-27 during the war and later played halfback for three years with the Chicago Bears. He went into coaching then, first as an assistant to George Halas in Chicago and then as head coach in the Missouri Valley Conference, the Big Eight and the Southeast Conference. He became famous for creating order out of chaos, building good teams at schools known for their perennial losers. He had four unbeaten seasons, five conference champions and two national champions. Then a second-string quarterback said or did something he didn't like and Creed broke his jaw. It became something of a national scandal and he went into obscurity for three years until Mrs. Tom beckoned him to west Texas. It was a long drop down from the Big Eight but Creed managed to convince the widow that a good football team could put her lonely little school on the map. So priorities were changed, new assistants were hired, alumni were courted, a certain amount of oil money began to flow, a certain number of private planes were made available for recruiting purposes, the team name was changed from the Cactus Wrens to the Screaming Eagles—and Emmett Creed was on the comeback trail. The only thing that didn't make sense was the ton of canvas that hid our practice sessions. There was nothing out there but insects.

The first unit was called back in and I headed slowly toward the dust and noise. Creed up in the tower spoke through his bullhorn.

"Defense, I'd appreciate some pursuit. They don't give points for apathy in this sport. Pursue those people. Come out of the ground at them. Hit somebody. Hit somebody. Hit somebody."

On the first play Garland Hobbs, our quarterback, faked to me going straight into the line and then pitched to the other setback, Jim Deering. He got hit first by a linebacker, Dennis Smee, who drove him into the ground, getting some belated and very nasty help from a tackle and another linebacker. Deering didn't move. Two assistant coaches started shouting at him, telling him he was defacing the landscape. He tried to get up but couldn't make it. The rest of us walked over to the far hashmark and ran the next play.

It all ended with two laps around the goal posts. Lloyd Philpot Jr., a defensive end, fell down in the middle of the second lap. We left him there in the end zone, on his stomach, one leg twitching slightly. His father had won all-conference honors at Baylor for three straight years.

That evening Emmett Creed addressed the squad.

"Write home on a regular basis. Dress neatly. Be courteous. Articulate your problems. Do not drag-ass. Anything I have no use for, it's a football player who consistently drag-asses. Move swiftly from place to place, both on the field and in the corridors of buildings. Don't ever get too proud to pray."

3

ROLF HAUPTFUHRER COACHED the defensive line and attended to problems of morale and grooming. He approached me one morning after practice.

"We want you to room with Bloomberg," he said.

"Why me?"

"John Billy Small was in there with him. Couldn't take the tension. We figure you won't mind. You're more the complicated type."

"Of course I'll mind."

"John Billy said he wets the bed. Aside from that there's no problem. He gets nervous. No doubt about that. A lot of tension in that frame. But we figure you can cope with it."

"I object. I really do. I've got my own tensions."

"Harkness, everybody knows what kind of reputation you brought down here. Coach is willing to take a chance on you only as long as you follow orders. So keep in line. Just keep in line—hear?"

"Who's rooming with Taft Robinson?" I said.

"Robinson rooms alone."

"Why's that?"

"You'll have to ask the powers that be. In the meantime move your stuff in with Bloomberg."

"I don't like tension," I said. "And I don't see why I have to be the one who gets put in with controversial people."

"It's for the good of the team," Hauptfuhrer said.

Five of us sneaked into the nearest town that night, a

place called Rooster, to see what was happening. We ended up at Bing Jackmin's house, right outside town, where we drank beer for five hours. Bing's father joined us, falling off the porch when he came out to say good night. We drove back to campus and held a drunken Olympiad in the moonlight at the edge of the football field—slow-motion races, grass swimming, spitting for distance. Then we walked slowly back to the dorm and listened to Norgene Azamanian tell the story of his name.

"A lot of people take it for a girl's name. But it's no such thing. It comes from Norge refrigerators and from my uncle, Captain Gene Kinney. How it all came about, my being called Norgene, makes for a real interesting story. You see, everybody in my mother's family going back for generations, man or woman, always had a Christian name of just one syllable. Nobody knows how it started but at some point along the line they decided they'd keep it going. So I go and get born and it comes time to name me. Now it just so happens there was an old Norge refrigerator out on the back porch waiting to get thrown away. It also happens that my daddy wasn't too happy about the syllable thing, it being his belief that the bible carries a warning against one-syllable names, Cain being his brother's slayer. And finally there was the amazing coincidence that my uncle Gene Kinney was on leave and coming over to visit so he could see the new baby, which was me, and so he could get in on the naming of it to be sure the family tradition would be carried out. How all these different factors resulted in the name Norgene is the whole crux of the story."

"Very good," Bing said. "But first tell us how you got Azamanian."

I went up to my room. Bloomberg was asleep, on his belly, snoring softly into the pillow. He was absolutely enormous. It was easy to imagine him attached to the bed by guy-wires, to be floated aloft once a year like a Macy's balloon. His full name was Anatole Bloomberg and he played left tackle on offense. That was all I knew about him, that plus the fact that he wasn't a Texan. One of the outcasts, I thought. Or a voluntary exile of the philosophic type. I decided to wake him up.

"Anatole," I said. "It's Gary Harkness, your new roommate. Let's shake hands and be friends."

"We're roommates," he said. "Why do we have to be friends?"

"It's just an expression. I didn't mean undying comrades. Just friends as opposed to enemies. I'm sorry I woke you up."

"I wasn't asleep."

"You were snoring," I said.

"That's the way I breathe when I'm on my stomach. What happened to my original roommate?"

"John Billy? John Billy's been moved."

"Was that his name?"

"He's been moved. I hope you're not tense about my showing up. All I want to do is get off to a good start and avoid all possible tension."

"Who in your opinion was the greater man?" Bloomberg said. "Edward Gibbon or Archimedes?"

"Archimedes."

"Correct," he said.

In the morning Creed sent us into an all-out scrimmage with a brief inspirational message that summed up everything we knew or had to know.

"It's only a game," he said, "but it's the only game."

Taft Robinson and I were the setbacks. Taft caught a flare pass, evaded two men and went racing down the sideline, Bobby Iselin, a cornerback, gave up the chase at the 25. Bobby used to be the team's fastest man.

4

THROUGH ALL OUR DAYS together my father returned time and again to a favorite saying.

"Suck in that gut and go harder."

He never suggested that this saying of his ranked with the maxims of Teddy Roosevelt. Still, he was dedicated to it. He believed in the idea that a simple but lasting reward, something just short of a presidential handshake, awaited the extra effort, the persevering act of a tired man. Backbone, will, mental toughness, desire—these were his themes, the qualities that insured success. He was a pharmaceutical salesman with a lazy son.

It seems that wherever I went I was hounded by people urging me to suck in my gut and go harder. They would never give up on me—my father, my teachers, my coaches, even a girl friend or two. I was a challenge, I guess: a piece of string that does not wish to be knotted. My father was by far the most tireless of those who tried to give me direction, to sharpen my initiative, to piece together some collective memory of hard-won land or dusty struggles in the sun. He put a sign in my room.

WHEN THE GOING GETS TOUGH
THE TOUGH GET GOING

I looked at this sign for three years (roughly from ages fourteen to seventeen) before I began to perceive a certain beauty in it. The sentiment of course had small appeal but it seemed that beauty flew from the words themselves, the letters, consonants swallowing vowels, aggression and tenderness, a semi-self-re-creation from line to line, word to word, letter to letter. All meaning faded. The words became pictures. It was a sinister thing to discover at such an age, that words can escape their meanings. A strange beauty that sign began to express.

My father had a territory and a company car. He sold vitamins, nutritional supplements, mineral preparations, and antibiotics. His customers included about fifty doctors and dentists, about a dozen pharmacies, a few hospitals, some drug wholesalers. He had specific goals, both geographic and economic, each linked with the other, and perhaps because of this he hated waste of any kind, of shoe leather, talent, irretrievable time. (Get cracking. Straighten out. Hang in.) It paid, in his view, to follow the simplest, most pioneer of rhythms—the eternal work cycle, the blood-hunt for bear and deer, the mellow rocking of chairs as screen doors swing open and bang shut in the gathering fragments of summer's sulky dusk. Beyond these honest latitudes lay nothing but chaos.

He had played football at Michigan State. He had ambitions on my behalf and more or less at my expense. This is the custom among men who have failed to be heroes; their sons must prove that the seed was not impoverished. He had spent his autumn Saturdays on the sidelines, watching others fall in battle and rise then to the thunder of the drums and the crowd's demanding chants. He put me in a football uniform very early. Then, as a high school junior, I won all-state honors at halfback. (This was the first of his ambitions and as it turned out the only one to be fulfilled.) Eventually I received twenty-eight offers of athletic scholarships—tuition, books, room and board, fifteen dollars a month. There were several broad hints of further almsgiving. Visions were painted of lovely young ladies with charitable instincts of their own. It seemed that every section of the country had much to offer in the way of scenery, outdoor activities, entertainment, companionship, and even, if necessary, education.

On the application blanks, I had to fill in my height, my weight, my academic average and my time for the 40-yard dash.

I handed over a letter of acceptance to Syracuse University. I was eager to enrich their tradition of great running backs. They threw me out when I barricaded myself in my room with two packages of Oreo cookies and a girl named Lippy Margolis. She wanted to hide from the world and I volunteered to help her. For a day and a night we read to each other from a textbook on economics. She seemed calmed by the incoherent doctrines set forth on those pages. When I was sure I had changed the course of her life for the better, I opened the door.

At Penn State, the next stop, I studied hard and played well. But each day that autumn was exactly like the day before and the one to follow. I had not yet learned to appreciate the slowly gliding drift of identical things; chunks of time spun past me like meteorites in a universe predicated on repetition. For weeks the cool clear weather was unvarying; the girls wore white knee-high stockings; a small red plane passed over the practice field every afternoon at the same time. There was something hugely Asian about those days in Pennsylvania. I tripped on the same step on the same staircase on three successive days. After this I stopped going to practice. The freshman coach wanted to know what was up. I told him I knew all the plays; there was no reason to practice them over and over; the endless repetition might be spiritually disastrous; we were becoming a nation devoted to human xerography. He and I had a long earnest discussion. Much was made of my talent and my potential value to the varsity squad. Oneness was stressed—the oneness necessary for a winning team. It was a good concept, oneness, but I suggested that, to me at least, it could not be truly attractive unless it meant oneness with God or the universe or some equally redoubtable super-phenomenon. What he meant by oneness was in fact elevenness or twenty-twoness. He told me that my attitude was all wrong. People don't go to football games to see pass patterns run by theologians. He told me, in effect, that I would have to suck in my gut and go harder. (1) A team sport. (2) The need to sacrifice. (3) Preparation for the future. (4) Microcosm of life.

"You're saying that what I learn on the gridiron about sacrifice and oneness will be of inestimable value later on in life. In other words if I give up now I'll almost surely give up in the more important contests of the future."

"That's it exactly, Gary."

"I'm giving up," I said.

It was a perverse thing to do—go home and sit through a blinding white winter in the Adirondacks. I was passing through one of those odd periods of youth in which significance is seen only on the blankest of walls, found only in dull places, and so I thought I'd turn my back to the world and to my father's sign and try to achieve, indeed establish, some lowly form of American sainthood. The repetition of Penn State was small stuff compared to that deep winter. For five months I did nothing and then repeated it. I had breakfast in the kitchen, lunch in my room, dinner at the dinner table with the others, meaning my parents. They concluded that I was dying of something slow and incurable and that I did not wish to tell them in order to spare their feelings. This was an excellent thing to infer for all concerned. My father took down the sign and hung in its place a framed photo of his favorite pro team, the Detroit Lions—their official team picture. In late spring, a word appeared all over town. MILITARIZE. The word was printed on cardboard placards that stood in shop windows. It was scrawled on fences. It was handwritten on loose-leaf paper taped to the windshields of cars. It appeared on bumper stickers and signboards.

I had accomplished nothing all those months and so I decided to enroll at the University of Miami. It wasn't a bad place. Repetition gave way to the beginnings of simplicity. (A preparation thus for Texas) I wanted badly to stay. I liked playing football and I knew that by this time

I'd have trouble finding another school that would take me. But I had to leave. It started with a book, an immense volume about the possibilities of nuclear war—assigned reading for a course I was taking in modes of disaster technology. The problem was simple and terrible: I enjoyed the book. I liked reading about the deaths of tens of millions of people. I liked dwelling on the destruction of great cities. Five to twenty million dead. Fifty to a hundred million dead. Ninety percent population loss. Seattle wiped out by mistake. Moscow demolished. Airbursts over every SAC base in Europe. I liked to think of huge buildings toppling, of firestorms, of bridges collapsing, survivors roaming the charred countryside. Carbon 14 and strontium 90. Escalation ladder and subcrisis situation. Titan, Spartan, Poseidon. People burned and unable to breathe. People being evacuated from doomed cities. People diseased and starving. Two hundred thousand bodies decomposing on the roads outside Chicago. I read several chapters twice. Pleasure in the contemplation of millions dying and dead. I became fascinated by words and phrases like thermal hurricane, overkill, circular error probability, post-attack environment, stark deterrence, dose-rate contours, kill-ratio, spasm war. Pleasure in these words. They were extremely effective, I thought, whispering shyly of cycles of destruction so great that the language of past world wars became laughable, the wars themselves somewhat naive. A thrill almost sensual accompanied the reading of this book. What was wrong with me? Had I gone mad? Did others feel as I did? I became seriously depressed. Yet I went to the library and got more books on the subject. Some of these had been published well after the original volume and things were much more up-to-date. Old weapons vanished. Megatonnage soared. New concepts appeared—the rationality of irrationality, hostage cities, orbital attacks. I became more fascinated, more depressed, and finally I left Coral Gables and went back home to my room and to the official team photo of the Detroit Lions. It seemed the only thing to do. My mother brought lunch upstairs. I took the dog for walks.

In time the draft board began to get interested. I allowed my father to get in touch with a former classmate of his, an influential alumnus of Michigan State. Negotiations were held and I was granted an interview with two subalterns of the athletic department, types familiar to football and other paramilitary complexes, the square-jawed bedrock of the corporation. They knew what I could do on the football field, having followed my high school career, but they wouldn't accept me unless I could convince them that I was ready to take orders, to pursue a mature course, to submit my will to the common good. I managed to convince them. I went to East Lansing the following autumn, an aging recruit, and was leading the freshman squad in touchdowns, yards gained rushing, and platitudes. Then, in a game against the Indiana freshmen, I was one of three players converging on a safetyman who had just intercepted a pass. We seemed to hit him simultaneously. He died the next day and I went home that evening.

I stayed in my room for seven weeks this time, shuffling a deck of cards. I got to the point where I could cut to the six of spades about three out of five times, as long as I didn't try it too often, abuse the gift, as long as I tried only when I truly felt an emanation from the six, when I knew in my fingers that I could cut to that particular card.

Then I got a phone call from Emmett Creed. Two days later he flew up to see me. I liked the idea of losing myself in an obscure part of the world. And I had discovered a very simple truth. My life meant nothing without football.

5

RAYMOND TOON STOOD six feet seven. He was a mild young man, totally unintimidating, a former bible student. He was a reserve tackle on defense and he had come here because it was the only school he knew of that offered a course in sportscasting.

"Time-adjusted rate of return," he said. "Redundant asset method. Capital budgeting. Probable stream of earnings. Independently negotiated credit balances. Consolidation. Tax anticipation notes."

We were in the cafeteria. John Jessup was also at our table, reading a textbook. Jessup and Toon were roommates. Jessup didn't like the arrangement because Raymond practiced his sportscasting in the room all weekend. When he wasn't studying theories of economic valuation, he was camped in front of his portable TV set. He'd switch it on, turn the sound down to nothing, and describe the action. At this time of year it was mainly baseball, golf, bowling and stock car racing. Jessup had complained to Rolf Hauptfuhrer that he was being driven out of his mind. But so far nothing had been done. Moody Kimbrough brought his tray over to our table.

"This milk is putrid," Jessup told him.

"What do you want from me?"

"You're one of the captains. Go tell Coach. They shouldn't give us milk like this. They should be more careful with the athletes' milk."

"Back home it's the blankety-blank water you have to watch," Kimbrough said.

"Back where I come from it's the water and the milk," Raymond said.

"This is shitpiss," Jessup said. "This is the worst-ass milk I ever tasted."

Kimbrough drank from his little carton.

"I'll tell you something," he said. "This milk is putrid."

"Damnright," Jessup said.

"This milk is contaminated. It's putrid. It's the worst I ever tasted. Back up home it's the water. Here I guess it's the milk. I'll be sure and tell Coach."

"Toony, what was the point you were trying to make?" I said.

"The level of deemed merit," Raymond said. "Assessed value. Imputed market prices. Munitions. Maximized comparative risk."

Onan Moley joined us. He was wearing a sweat shirt with a screaming eagle, the team symbol, pictured across the front. The word SACRIFICE was inscribed beneath the eagle. Onan hunched his shoulders and lowered his head almost to table level before speaking.

"There's a lot of talk about a lot of things."

"What talk?" Kimbrough said.

"Never mind."

"I'm co-captain, Onan. I've got a pipeline. But I don't know about any talk. Now what talk do you mean?"

"There might be a queer on the squad."

"Offense or defense," Kimbrough said.

Terry Madden seated himself at the end of the table. He broke a roll and began to butter it.

"What's the good word?" he said.

Jessup read aloud from his textbook on monolithic integrated circuitry.

"The pattern match begins with a search for a substring of a given string that has a specified structure in the string-manipulation language."

Taft Robinson was sitting three tables away. I took my dessert over. He looked up, nodded, then looked down

again and sliced a quivering ribbon of fat off the last piece
of sirloin on his plate.

"That weak-side sweep looked good today," I said. "I
finally got in a good block for you."

"I saw it," he said.

"I wiped out that bastard Smee. He likes to hurt people, that son of a bitch."

"Which one is he?"

"Middle linebacker. He's the defensive captain. He
captains the defense."

"I saw the block," Taft said.

"I really wiped him out, that bastard. Hey, look, what
are you doing here anyway?"

"Where—here?"

"Right," I said. "Here in this particular locale. This
dude ranch."

"I'm here to play football. Same as you."

"You could be at almost any school in the country.
Why would you want to leave a place like Columbia to
come here? Granted, Columbia's not exactly a football
colossus. But to come here. How the hell did you let
Creed talk you into this place? It's not as though you're
integrating the place. Technically you're integrating the
place but that's only because nobody else ever wanted to
come here. Who the hell would want to come to a place
like this?"

"You came here."

"Hey, Robinson," Kimbrough said.

"I'm here because I'm a chronic ballbreaker. First, it's
not likely any other school would have me. Second, I
wanted to disappear."

"But you're here," he said. "We're all here."

"I can't argue with that. How's your milk? Jessup says
the milk is putrid."

"Which one is he?"

"Hey, Robinson," Moody Kimbrough said. "We don't
wear sunglasses indoors around here. We don't do that—
hear?"

"Mind your own business," I said.

I watched him coming toward our table. I thought briefly about the fact that he outweighed me by forty pounds or so. Then I got up and hit him in the stomach. He made a noise, an abrupt burp, and hit me in roughly the same spot. I sat down and tried to breathe. When I raised my head finally, Taft was just finishing his dessert.

6

WE STOOD IN A CIRCLE in the enormous gray morning, all the receivers and offensive backs, helmets in hands. Thunder moved down from the northeast. Creed, in a transparent raincoat, was already up in the tower. At the center of the circle was Tom Cook Clark, an assistant coach, an expert on quarterbacking, known as a scholarly man because he smoked a pipe and did not use profanity.

"What we want to do is establish a planning procedures approach whereby we neutralize the defense. We'll be employing a lot of play-action and some pass-run options off the sweep. We'll be using a minimum number of sprint-outs because the passing philosophy here is based on the pocket concept and we don't want to inflate the injury potential which is what you do if your quarterback strays from the pocket and if he can't run real well, which most don't. We use the aerial game here to implement the ground game whereby we force their defense to respect the run which is what they won't do if they can anticipate pass and read pass and if our frequency, say on

second and long, indicates pass. So that's what we'll try to
come up with, depending on the situation and the con-
tingency plan and how they react to the running game. I
should insert at this point that if they send their linebackers, you've been trained and briefed and you know
how to counter this. You've got your screen, your flare,
your quick slant-in. You've been drilled and drilled on this
in the blitz drills. It all depends on what eventuates. It's
just eleven men doing their job. That's all it is."

Oscar Veech moved into the circle.

"I want you to bust ass out there today," he said.
"Guards and tackles, I want you to come off that ball real
quick and pop, pop, hit those people, move those people
out, pop them, put some hurt on them, drive them back
till they look like sick little puppy dogs squatting down to
crap."

"The guards and tackles are over in that other group,"
I said.

"Right, right, right. Now go out there and execute.
Move that ball. Hit somebody. Hit somebody. Hit somebody."

Garland Hobbs handed off to me on a quick trap and
two people hit me. There was a big pile-up and I felt a
fair number of knees and elbows and then somebody's
hand was inside my facemask trying to come away with
flesh. I realized Mr. Kimbrough had issued directives. On
the next play I was pass-blocking for Hobbs and they
sent everybody including the free safety. I went after the
middle linebacker, Dennis Smee, helmet to groin, and
then fell on top of him with a forearm leading the way.

Whistles were blowing and the coaches edged in a bit
closer. Vern Feck took off his baseball cap and put his
pink face right into the pile-up, little sparks of saliva
jumping out of his whistle as he blew it right under my
nose. Creed came down from the tower.

7

OF ALL THE ASPECTS of exile, silence pleased me least. Other things were not so displeasing. Exile compensates the banished by offering certain opportunities. Each day, for example, I spent some time in meditation. This never failed to be a lovely interlude, for there was nothing to meditate on. Each day I added a new word to my vocabulary, wrote a letter to someone I loved, and memorized the name of one more president of the United States and the years of his term in office. Simplicity, repetition, solitude, starkness, discipline upon discipline. There were profits here, things that could be used to make me stronger; the small fanatical monk who clung to my liver would thrive on such ascetic scraps. And then there was geography. We were in the middle of the middle of nowhere, that terrain so flat and bare, suggestive of the end of recorded time, a splendid sense of remoteness firing my soul. It was easy to feel that back up there, where men spoke the name civilization in wistful tones, I was wanted for some terrible crime.

Exile in a real place, a place of few bodies and many stones, is just an extension (a packaging) of the other exile, the state of being separated from whatever is left of the center of one's own history. I found comfort in west Texas. There was even pleasure in the daily punishment on the field. I felt that I was better for it, reduced in complexity, a warrior.

But the silence was difficult. It hung over the land and drifted across the long plains. It was out there with the soft black insects beyond the last line of buildings, beyond the prefabs and the Quonset hut and the ROTC barracks. Day after day my eyes scanned in all directions a stunned earth, unchangingly dull, a land silenced by its own beginnings in the roaring heat, born dead, flat stones burying the memory. I felt threatened by the silence. In my room at home, during my retreats from destructive episodes of one kind or another, I had never even noticed the quiet. Perhaps silence is dispersed by familiar things: their antiquity is heard. All I had feared then was that my mother, bringing my lunch upstairs, would forget to comment on the weather. (These reports were indispensable to my progress.) But now, in the vast burning west, the silences were menacing. I decided not to eat meat for a few weeks.

One day in early September we started playing a game called Bang You're Dead. It's an extremely simple-minded game. Almost every child has played it in one form or another. Your hand assumes the shape of a gun and you fire at anyone who passes. You try to reproduce, in your own way, the sound of a gun being fired. Or you simply shout these words: *Bang, you're dead*. The other person clutches a vital area of his body and then falls, simulating death. (Never mere injury; always death.) Nobody knew who had started the game or exactly when it had started. You had to fall if you were shot. The game depended on this.

It went on for six or seven days. At first, naturally enough, I thought it was all very silly, even for a bunch of bored and lonely athletes. Then I began to change my mind. Suddenly, beneath its bluntness, the game seemed compellingly intricate. It possessed gradations, dark joys, a resonance echoing from the most perplexing of dreams. I began to kill selectively. When killed, I fell to the floor or earth with great deliberation, with sincerity. I varied my falls, searching for the rhythm of something imperishable, a classic death.

We did not abuse the powers inherent in the game. The only massacre took place during the game's first or second day when things were still shapeless, the potential unrealized. It started on the second floor of the dormitory just before lights-out and worked along the floor and down one flight, everyone shooting each other, men in their underwear rolling down the stairs, huge nude brutes draped over the banisters. The pleasure throughout was empty. I guess we realized together that the game was better than this. So we cooled things off and devised unwritten limits.

I shot Terry Madden at sunset from a distance of forty yards as he appeared over the crest of a small hill and came toward me. He held his stomach and fell, in slow motion, and then rolled down the grassy slope, tumbling, rolling slowly as possible, closer, slower, ever nearer, tumbling down to die at my feet with the pale setting of the sun.

To kill with impunity. To die in the celebration of ancient ways.

All those days the almost empty campus was marked by the sound of human gunfire. There were several ways in which this sound was uttered—the comical, the truly gruesome, the futuristic, the stylized, the circumspect. Each served to break the silence of the long evenings. From the window of my room I'd hear the faint gunfire and see a lone figure in the distance fall to the ground. Sometimes, hearing nothing, I'd merely see the victim get hit, twisting around a tree as he fell or slowly dropping to his knees, and this isolated motion also served to break the silence, the lingering stillness of that time of day. So there was that reason above all to appreciate the game; it forced cracks in the enveloping silence.

I died well and for this reason was killed quite often. One afternoon, shot from behind, I staggered to the steps of the library and remained there, on my back, between the second and seventh step at the approximate middle of the stairway, for more than a few minutes. It was very relaxing despite the hardness of the steps. I felt the sun on my face. I tried to think of nothing. The longer I re-

mained there, the more absurd it seemed to get up. My
body became accustomed to the steps and the sun felt
warmer. I was completely relaxed. I felt sure I was alone,
that no one was standing there watching or even walking
by. This thought relaxed me even more. In time I opened
my eyes. Taft Robinson was sitting on a bench not far
away, reading a periodical. For a moment, in a state of
near rapture, I thought it was he who had fired the shot.

At length the rest of the student body reported for the
beginning of classes. We were no longer alone and the
game ended. But I would think of it with affection because of its scenes of fragmentary beauty, because it
brought men closer together through their perversity and
fear, because it enabled us to pretend that death could be
a tender experience, and because it breached the long
silence.

8

IT'S NOT EASY to fake a limp. The tendency is to exagger-
ate, a natural mistake and one that no coach would fail
to recognize. Over the years I had learned to eliminate
this tendency. I had mastered the dip and grimace, per-
fected the semi-moan, and when I came off the field this
time, after receiving a mild blow on the right calf, nobody
considered pressing me back into service. The trainer
handed me an ice pack and I sat on the bench next to
Bing Jackmin, who kicked field goals and extra points.
The practice field was miserably hot. I was relieved to be
off and slightly surprised that I felt guilty about it. Bing
Jackmin was wearing headgear; his eyes, deep inside the

facemask, seemed crazed by sun or dust or inner visions.

"Work," he shouted past me. "Work, you substandard industrial robots. Work, work, work, work."

"Look at them hit," I said. "What a pretty sight. When Coach says hit, we hit. It's so simple."

"It's not simple, Gary. Reality is constantly being interrupted. We're hardly even aware of it when we're out there. We perform like things with metal claws. But there's the other element. For lack of a better term I call it the psychomythical. That's a phrase I coined myself."

"I don't like it. What does it refer to?"

"Ancient warriorship," he said. "Cults devoted to pagan forms of technology. What we do out on that field harks back. It harks back. Why don't you like the term?"

"It's vague and pretentious. It means nothing. There's only one good thing about it. Nobody could remember a stupid phrase like that for more than five seconds. See, I've already forgotten it."

"Wuuurrrrk. Wuuuurrrrrk."

"Hobbs'll throw to Jessup now," I said. "He always goes to his tight end on third and short inside the twenty. He's like a retarded computer."

"For a quarterback Hobbs isn't too bright. But you should have seen him last year, Gary. At least Creed's got him changing plays at the line. Last year it was all Hobbsie could do to keep from upchucking when he saw a blitz coming. Linebackers pawing at the ground, snarling at him. He didn't have what you might call a whole lot of poise."

"Here comes Cecil off. Is that him?"

"They got old Cecil. Looks like his shoulder."

Cecil Rector, a guard, came toward the sideline and Roy Yellin went running in to replace him. The trainer popped Cecil's shoulder back into place. Then Cecil fainted. Bing strolled down that way to have a look at Cecil unconscious. Vern Feck, who coached the linebackers, started shouting at his people. Then he called the special units on to practice kickoff return and coverage. Bing headed slowly up to the 40-yard line. He kicked off and the two teams converged, everybody yelling, bodies rolling and bouncing on the scant grass. When it was over Bing came back to the bench. His eyes seemed to belong to some small dark cave animal.

"Something just happened," he said.

"You look frightened."

"You won't believe what just happened. I was standing out there, getting ready to stride toward the ball, when a strange feeling came over me. I was looking right at the football. It was up on the tee. I was standing ten yards away, looking right at it, waiting for the whistle so I could make my approach, and that's when I got this strange insight. I wish I could describe it, Gary, but it was too wild, too unbelievable. It was too everything, man. Nobody would understand what I meant if I tried to describe it."

"Describe it," I said.

"I sensed knowledge in the football. I sensed a strange power and restfulness. The football possessed awareness. The football knew what was happening. It knew. I'm sure of it."

"Are you serious, Bing?"

"The football knew that this is a football game. It knew that it was the center of the game. It was aware of its own footballness."

"But was it aware of its own awareness? That's the ultimate test, you know."

"Go ahead, Gary, play around. I knew you wouldn't understand. It was too unreal. It was un-everything, man."

"You went ahead and kicked the ball."

"Naturally," he said. "That's the essence of the word. It's a football, isn't it? It is a *foot ball*. My foot sought union with the ball."

We watched Bobby Hopper get about eighteen on a

sweep. When the play ended a defensive tackle named Dickie Kidd remained on his knees. He managed to take his helmet off and then fell forward, his face hitting the midfield stripe. Two players dragged him off and Raymond Toon went running in to replace him. The next play fell apart when Hobbs fumbled the snap. Creed spoke to him through the bullhorn. Bing walked along the bench to look at Dickie Kidd.

I watched the scrimmage. It was getting mean out there. The players were reaching the point where they wanted to inflict harm. It was hardly a time for displays of finesse and ungoverned grace. This was the ugly hour. I felt like getting back in. Bing took his seat again.

"How's Dickie?"

"Dehydration," Bing said. "Hauptfuhrer's giving him hell."

"What for?"

"For dehydrating."

I went over to Oscar Veech and told him I was ready. He said they wanted to take a longer look at Jim Deering. I watched Deering drop a short pass and get hit a full two seconds later by Buddy Shock, a linebacker. This cheered me up and I returned to the bench.

"They want to look at Deering some more."

"Coach is getting edgy. We open in six days. This is the last scrimmage and he wants to look at everybody."

"I wish I knew how good we are."

"Coach must be thinking the same thing."

Time was called and the coaches moved in to lecture their players. Creed climbed down from the tower and walked slowly toward Garland Hobbs. He took off his baseball cap and brushed it against his thigh as he walked. Hobbs saw him coming and instinctively put on his helmet. Creed engaged him in conversation.

"It's a tongue-lashing," Bing said. "Coach is hacking at poor old Hobbsie."

"He seems pretty calm."

"It's a tongue-lashing," Bing hissed to Cecil Rector, who was edging along the bench to sit next to us.

"How's the shoulder?" I said.

"Dislocated."

"Too bad."

"They can put a harness on it," he said. "We go in six days. If Coach needs me, I'll be ready."

Just then Creed looked toward Bing Jackmin, drawing him off the bench without even a nod. Bing jogged over there. The rest of the players were standing or kneeling between the 40-yard lines. Next to me, Cecil Rector leaned over and plucked at blades of grass. I thought of the Adirondacks, chill lakes of inverted timber, sash of blue snow across the mountains, the whispering presence of the things that filled my room. Far beyond the canvas blinds, on the top floor of the women's dormitory, a figure stood by an open window. I thought of women. I thought of women in snow and rain, on mountains and in forests, at the end of long galleries immersed in the brave light of Rembrandts.

"Coach is real anxious," Rector said. "He knows a lot of people are watching to see how he does. I bet the wire services send somebody out to cover the opener. If they can ever find this place."

"I'd really like to get back in."

"So would I," he said. "Yellin's been haunting me since way back last spring. He's like a hyena. Every time I get hurt, Roy Yellin is right there grinning. He likes to see me get hurt. He's after my job. Every time I'm face down on the grass in pain, I know I'll look up to see Roy Yellin grinning at the injured part of my body. His daddy sells mutual funds in the prairie states."

Bing came back, apparently upset about something.

"He wants me to practice my squib kick tomorrow. I told him I don't have any squib kick. He guaranteed me I'd have one by tomorrow night. Then he called Onan over and picked him apart. Told him he was playing center as if the position had just been invented."

"They're putting Randy King in for Onan," I said.

"Onan's been depressed," Bing said. "He found out his girl friend spent a night with some guy on leave from Nam. It's affecting his play."

"What did they do?" Rector said.

"They spent a night."

"Did they have relations?"

"Are you asking me did they fuck?"

"There goes Taft again," I said. "Look at that cutback. God, that's beautiful."

"He's some kind of football player."

"He's a real good one."

"He can do it all, can't he?"

They played for another fifteen minutes. On the final play, after a long steady drive that took the offense down to the 8-yard line, Taft fumbled the hand-off. Defense recovered, whistles blew, and that was it for the day. The three of us headed back together.

"Hobbsie laid it right in his gut and he goes and loses it," Rector said. "I attribute that kind of error to lack of concentration. That's a mental error and it's caused by lack of concentration. Coloreds can run and leap but they can't concentrate. A colored is a runner and leaper. You're making a big mistake if you ask him to concentrate."

A very heavy girl wearing an orange dress came walking toward us across a wide lawn. There was a mushroom cloud appliquéd on the front of her dress. I recognized the girl; we had some classes together. I let the others walk on ahead and I stood for a moment watching her walk past me and move into the distance. I was wearing a smudge of lampblack under each eye to reduce the sun's glare. I didn't know whether the lampblack was very effective but I liked the way it looked and I liked the idea of painting myself in a barbaric manner before going forth to battle in mud. I wondered if the fat girl knew I was still watching her. I had a vivid picture of myself standing there holding my helmet at my side, left knee bent slightly, hair all mussed and the lampblack under my eyes. Her dress was brightest orange. I thought she must be a little crazy to wear a dress like that with her figure.

9

THE THING TO DO, I thought, is to walk in circles. This is demanded by the mythology of all deserts and wasted places. A number of traditions insist on it. I was about a mile beyond the campus. Motion was strange. Motion consisted of sunlight on particular stones. (With the opening of classes I had been brushing up on perimeter acquisition radar, unauthorized explosions, slow-motion counter-city war, super-ready status, collateral destruction, crisis management, civilian devastation attack.) All the colors were different shades of one nameless color. Water would have been a miracle or mirage. I took off my shoes and socks and the stones burned. I saw a long bug. I was careful to keep the tallest of the campus buildings in sight. This was a practical measure, nonritualistic, meant to offset the saintly feet. I remembered then to think of Rutherford B. Hayes, nineteenth president, 1877–1881. That took care of that for the day. Each day had to be completed. I avoided a sharp stone. Something sudden, a movement, turned out to be sunlight on paint, a painted stone, one stone, black in color, identifiably black, a single round stone, painted black, carefully painted, the ground around it the same nameless color as the rest of the plain. Some vandal had preceded me then. Stone-painter. Metaphorist of the desert. To complete the day truly I had to remember to think of Milwaukee in flames. I was doing a different area every day. This practice filled me with self-disgust and was meant, eventually, to liberate me from the joy of imagining millions dead. In time, I assumed, my disgust would become so great that I would be released from all sense of global holocaust. But it wasn't working. I continued to look forward to each new puddle of destruction. Six megatons for Cairo. MIRVs for the Benelux countries. Typhoid and cholera for the Hudson River Valley. I seemed to be subjecting my emotions to an unintentioned cycle in which pleasure nourished itself on the black bones of revulsion and dread. Tidal waves for Bremerhaven. Long-term radiation for the Mekong Delta. For Milwaukee I had planned firestorms. But now I could not imagine Milwaukee in flames. I had never been to Milwaukee. I had never even seen a photograph of the place. I had no idea what the city looked like and I could not imagine it in flames. I put on my socks first, as I had been taught, and then my shoes. I was hungry. Pot roast had been served for lunch and I had eaten only some cereal and fruit. Heading back I kept watching for insects. Buildings rose across the plain. I could see cadets marching quite clearly now, bright blue squadrons on the parade grounds. The thing to do is to concentrate on objects. In the room, when I got there, Bloomberg was occupying his bed, prone, on top of the blanket, hands folded behind his white neck—the lone unsuntanned member of the squad. There were two beds, two chairs, two desks, a window, a closet. His white skin was remarkable. Some dietary law perhaps. An overhead light, two wall lamps. Consume only those foods that do not tint the flesh. A desk lamp, two bureaus, a wastebasket, a pencil, six books, three shoes. Bloomberg himself. Harkness himself or itself.

"Milwaukee is spared," I said.

10

HOURS LATER, after we had both missed dinner, Bloomberg rolled over on his back. He managed this without taking his hands from their position behind his neck. He used his elbows as levers and brakes, as landing gear. It seemed some kind of test—to move one's body 180 degrees without changing the relationship among its parts. Finally he settled himself and stared into the ceiling. I was sitting on my own bed, my back against the wall. This placing of bodies may seem inconsequential. But I believed it mattered terribly where we were situated and which way we were facing. Words move the body into position. In time the position itself dictates events. As the sun went down I tried to explain this concept to Bloomberg.

"History is guilt," he said.

"It's also the placement of bodies. What men say is relevant only to the point at which language moves masses of people or a few momentous objects into significant juxtaposition. After that it becomes almost mathematical. The placements take over. It becomes some sort of historical calculus. What you and I say this evening won't add up to much. We'll remember only where we sat, which way our feet pointed, at what angle our realities met. Whatever importance this evening might have is based on placements, relative positions, things like that. A million pilgrims face Mecca. Think of the power behind that fact. All turning now. And bending. And praying. History is the angle at which realities meet."

"History is guilt. It's mostly guilt."

"What are you doing here, Anatole?"

"I'm unjewing myself."

"I had a hunch. I thought to myself Anatole's being here has some spiritual import. It must be a hard thing to do. No wonder you're so tense."

"I'm not tense."

"You didn't even go down to dinner tonight. You're too tense to eat. It's quite obvious."

"I'm trying to lose weight," he said. "I'm like a bridge. I expand in hot weather. Creed wants to get me down to two seventy-five."

"Where are you now?"

"An even three."

"Don't you sweat it off in the grass drills or when we scrimmage?"

"I expand in this weather."

"Anatole, how do you unjew yourself?"

"You go to a place where there aren't any Jews. After that you revise your way of speaking. You take out the urbanisms. The question marks. All that folk wisdom. The melodies in your speech. The inverted sentences. You use a completely different set of words and phrases. Then you transform your mind into a ruthless instrument. You teach yourself to reject certain categories of thought."

"Why don't you want to be Jewish anymore?"

"I'm tired of the guilt. That enormous nagging historical guilt."

"What guilt?"

"The guilt of being innocent victims."

"Let's change the subject."

"Also the predicate and the object," he said.

He did not modify his expression. He seemed sublimely sad, a man engaged in surviving persistent winters at some northernmost point of the compass. I thought that winter must be his season, as it was mine, and it did not seem strange that we had come to this place. Even now, long before the snows, there was some quality of winter here, converse seasons almost interspersed, a sense of brevity, one color, much of winter's purity and silence, a chance for reason to prevail.

"Anatole, do you ever think of playing pro ball?"

"I'm not quick enough. I don't have quick feet. Tweego keeps after me about my feet. He says I'd be the best pass-blocker in the country if I had quick feet."

"I'd like to play pro ball," I said. "That would really be tremendous."

"You could make it, Gary."

"I don't have the speed. I'll never be big enough to go inside time after time, twenty-five or thirty times a game. And I don't have the speed to turn the corner. Up there you need overdrive. It would be tremendous if I could make it. It's tremendous just thinking about it."

"There are Jews in those big cities," Bloomberg said.

The window was open and there was a breeze. We were speaking very slowly, almost drunkenly. Our words seemed to rise toward the ceiling. The air was light and sweet. The words we spoke did not seem particularly ours; although we said nothing remarkable, the words surprised me at times. It may have been my hunger that accounted for these feelings.

"What's it like to weigh three hundred pounds?"

"It's like being an overwritten paragraph."

"They should get you a larger bed."

"I don't mind the bed. Everything is fine here. Things are going very well. I'm glad I came. It was good thinking. It showed intelligence. The bed is perfectly all right."

"Does the silence bother you?"

"What silence?" he said.

"You know what I mean. The big noise out there."

"Out over the desert you mean. The rumble."

"The silence. The big metallic noise."

"It doesn't bother me."

"It bothers me," I said.

I was enjoying myself immensely. I was drunk with

hunger. My tongue emitted wisdom after wisdom. Our words floated in the dimness, in the room's mild moonlight, weightless phrases polished by the cool confident knowledge of centuries. I was eager for subjects to envelop, timeless questions demanding men of antic dimension, riddles as yet unsolved, large bloody meat-hunks we might rip apart with mastiff teeth. Nothing unromantic would suffice. Detachment was needed only for the likes of astrophysics, quantum mechanics, all painstaking matters so delicate in their refracted light that intellects such as ours would sooner yield to the prudish machine. There was no vulgarity in the sciences of measurement, nothing to laugh at, to drink to, to weep about like Russians guzzling vodka and despairing of God a hundred years ago in books written by bearded titans. Bloomberg and I needed men, mass consciousness, great vulgar armies surging dumbly across the plains. Bloomberg weighed three hundred pounds. This itself was historical. I revered his weight. It was an affirmation of humanity's reckless potential; it went beyond legend and returned through mist to the lovely folly of history. To weigh three hundred pounds. What devout vulgarity. It seemed a worthwhile goal for prospective saints and flagellants. The new asceticism. All the visionary possibilities of the fast. To feed on the plants and animals of earth. To expand and wallow. I cherished his size, the formlessness of it, the sheer vulgar pleasure, his sense of being overwritten prose. Somehow it was the opposite of death.

"Feet retain the qualities they possessed at birth," Bloomberg said. "They're either quick or they're slow and there's nothing you can do about it. Tweego knows this. But he keeps after me anyway."

"Tweego is half-man, half-pig. All Creed's assistants have their piggish aspects but Tweego heads the list. He's fully half-pig. Tweego, Vern Feck and Hauptfuhrer. Mythology chose to ignore the species."

"I respect Tweego in a way. He thinks in one direction, straight ahead. He just aims and fires. He has ruthlessness of mind. That's something I respect. I think it's a distinctly modern characteristic. The systems planner. The management consultant. The nuclear stragegist. It's a question of fantastic single-mindedness. That's something I genuinely respect."

"It's all angles," I said. "The angle at which great masses collide. The angle at which projectiles are aimed. The angle at which blunt instruments strike a particular surface. Consider our respective positions."

"Go ahead, I'm listening."

"Consider the placements. Foot to hip. Knee to ear. Angles within angles. Interrelationships. The angle of incidence. The angle of reflection. Of course I'm just beginning to formulate this concept."

"Where do you do your thinking, Gary?"

"I've been spending time in the desert lately. You can evolve theories out there. The sun's heat purifies the thinking apparatus. Which reminds me. Why are you so white, Anatole? I've been reluctant to ask."

"I stay out of the sun whenever possible because I don't like to peel. I hate the whole process. Let's just say that my awareness of reptilian antecedents is unnaturally vivid."

"I like to peel," I said. "I like to reach behind me and strip the skin off my back. Or have it stripped off for me. A girl I knew in Coral Gables used to do it. Slowly peel the skin right off my back. She was Jewish."

"Did she make sounds while she did it?"

"Noises," I said. "She made noises."

Bloomberg shifted on the bed.

"I'm hungry," he said. "They had chicken for dinner. Fried chicken, mixed vegetables and corn bread. They had peach pie for dessert."

"Anatole, I think you should forget your diet. You'd be a better football player at two seventy-five. But a greater man at three hundred plus."

"It's possible but not probable. I base my notion of probability on a given number in a given pattern expressing the likelihood of the occurrence of a sequentially ordered set of events, such as the ratio of the number of coordinate elements that would produce the set of events to the total number of elements considered possible."

"I look forward to these talks of ours, chaplain."

At Logos there existed both Army and Air Force ROTC. I belonged to neither. But I had received permission to audit AFROTC courses. Geopolitics—one hour a week. History of air power—one hour a week. Aspects of modern war—one hour a week.

11

BOBBY LUKE WAS SITTING on the front steps of Staley Hall, the living quarters for the football team. It was another hot and empty afternoon; everybody else was indoors; the campus seemed deserted. I sat a few feet away from Bobby, spreading my arms along the top step. He looked my way with a slight grin, his eyes nearly shut. I stretched my legs and gazed out at the distant parade grounds. Nothing moved out there and the heat rolled in. The night before, we had opened against a school called Dorothy Hamilton Hodge. Taft Robinson gained 104 yards rushing in the first half and we left the field leading 24–0. Creed didn't use his reserves until there were only five minutes left in the game. By that time we had eight touchdowns; apparently he wanted to make news. Since Dorothy Hamilton Hodge was considered a typical opponent (with one exception), it was obvious that we'd have a winning season. We were better than any of us had imagined and it just seemed a question of how many points we'd score, how few we'd give up, and how many records would fall to Taft Robinson. The exception was West Centrex Biotechnical, an independent like us and a minor power in the area for years. The previous season they had swept through their schedule without the slightest hint of defeat, yielding an occasional touchdown only as a concession to the law of averages. The game with Centrex, which would be our seventh, was already shaping up as the whole season for us. If we could beat them, Creed's face would be back in the papers, we'd get small-college ranking, and the pro scouts would come drifting down for a look at the big old country boys. Bobby glanced up now. A side door of the science building had opened. A girl stepped out, stood for a moment with her arms folded, then went back in.

"Snatch," Bobby said.

The sky roared for a second. I looked up and saw it finally, a fighter, sunlight at its wingtips, climbing, lost now in the middle of the clear day. Bobby tried to spit past his shoes but didn't make it, hitting the left pants leg. Saliva hung there, glistening, full of exuberant bubbles. Bobby hummed a bit. I listened, trying to pick out a tune of some kind. Bobby was a strange sort of kid, lean but strong, a very sleepy violence radiating from his sparse body. He was famous for saying he would go through a brick wall for Coach Creed. Young athletes were always saying that sort of thing about their coaches. But Bobby became famous for it because he said practically nothing else. He was simply a shy boy who had little to say. Even the brick-wall remark was reserved for close friends in situations that called for earnestness above all else. We had all heard about it though, how often he used it, and I tried to figure out exactly what it meant to him. Maybe he had heard others use it and thought it was a remark demanded by history, a way of affirming the meaning of one's struggle. Maybe the words were commissioned, as it were, by language itself, by that compartment of language in which are kept all bits of diction designed to outlive the men who abuse them, all phrases that reduce speech to units of sounds, lullabies processed through intricate systems. Or maybe the remark just satisfied Bobby's need to be loyal to someone. Creed had done plenty to command respect but little or nothing to merit loyalty, a much more emotional quality. He kept to himself, using his assistants to temper and bend us, coming down from the tower only to correct a correction, living alone in a small room off the isometrics area—a landlocked Ahab who paced and raged, who was unfolding his life toward a single moment. Coach wanted our obedience and that was all. But Bobby had this loyalty to give, this eager violence of the heart, and he would smash his body to manifest it. Tradition, of course, supported his sense of what was right. The words were old and true, full of reassurance, comfort, consolation. Men followed such words to their death because other men before them had done the same, and perhaps it was easier to die than admit that words could lose their meaning. Bobby stopped humming now and tried to spit past his shoes again. The sun was directly overhead. Sunlight covered everything. I smelled casual sweat collecting under my arms and soon the soreness in my body began to ease just slightly. Two girls left the administration building and walked slowly across campus toward the women's dormitory. It took about ten minutes and we watched them all the way.

"Gash," Bobby said.

In time I let my head ease back on the top step and I closed my eyes. I was moving into the biblical phase of the afternoon, the peak of my new simplicity. A verity less than eternal had little appeal. I prepared myself to think of night, desert, sorrowful forests, of the moon, the stars, the west wind, baptismal mist and the rich myrrh of harvested earth. Instead I thought of tits. I thought of flaming limbs, a moody whore's mouth, hair the color of bourbon. Quietly I sweated, motionless on the steps. A girl in a cotton dress on a bed with brass posts. A ceiling fan rubbing the moist air. Scent of slick magazines. She'd be poorborn, the dumbest thing in Texas, a girl from a gulf town, movie-made, her voice an unlaundered drawl, fierce and coarse, fit for bad-tempered talking blues. I listened to Bobby hum. I had forgotten to add a new word to my vocabulary that day and I resolved to do it before nightfall. I tried to get back to the girl again. It was a different one this time, roundish, more than plump, almost monumental in her measureless dimensions. She removed her tessellated blue-green sweater. It was all happening in a Mexico City hotel. I heard Bobby stir. The girl became the hotel itself, an incredible cake of mosaic stone. I continued to perspire quietly. Women came and went, a few I'd known, some more magical than that, not memories and therefore absurdly sensual, exaggerated by cameras. It was wonderful to sit in one's own sweat and feel it bathe the tight muscles, tickling at this or that crevice, and to grow slightly delirious in the terrible sun and think of a woman's body (women in warm climates), someone to know when the room at the back of the house is damp and black until she is in it, the round one now, a quite unlikely woman to take you through this first silent winter, body of perfect knowledge, the flesh made word. Then I heard Bobby Luke scratching at his belly or neck.

"Pussy," he said.

I opened my eyes and searched the silent lawns.

12

WE WERE DOING simple calisthenics, row upon row of us, bending, breathing and stretching, instructing our collective soul in the disciplines necessary to make us one body, a thing of ninety legs. Two of the coaches, George Owen and Brian Tweego, walked through the ranks, bestowing their shrill blessing on prince and dog alike. At Tweego's command we switched to squat-jumps. Automatically my teammates groaned and just as automatically I became elated. My body surged and dropped; my mind repeated the process. The indifferent drift of time and all things filled me with affection for the universe. I squatted and jumped and jumped and squatted. Life was simplified by these afternoons of opposites and affinities. Eventually we headed toward the far goal posts for the first of two laps. I ran in a group that included Buddy Shock, Tim Flanders and Howard Lowry. When we were finished we watched the offensive linemen charge the blocking sled. These were Tweego's people and he screamed at them as he rode the sled, reviling Bloomberg and Onan Moley in particular. Creed himself stood about twenty yards off to the side, arms folded, eyes very busy beneath the peak of his black baseball cap.

"Coach is a man of destiny," Tim Flanders said. "They're a vanishing breed. My grandfather was a man of destiny. On my father's side. His whole identity was dominated by some tremendous vision."

"Identity," Buddy Shock said. "An equality satisfied by all possible values of the variables for which the stan-

dardized expressions involved in the equality are quanti-
tatively determined."

"What happened to your grandfather?" I said.

"He was killed in an industrial accident," Flanders
said. "He was burned beyond recognition. Selective ord-
nance. You know what that is, don't you?"

"You're not saying that was his destiny. To get burned
beyond recognition."

"Of course not."

"Then what was his destiny?"

"He never attained it, Gary. It was the accident that
prevented him from attaining it."

"Then how do you know he was a man of destiny?"

"Same way I know Coach is a man of destiny. He sits
up nights. He has piercing eyes. You never see him in a
phone booth."

Garland Hobbs strolled over to join us. He was tall and
solidly constructed, about six-four and 215, good-looking
in a blank way, faintly impressive, like a tall motel. He
had a quarterback's gait, slack and expensive.

"What's your comment on the big move?" I said.

"What move is that?"

"Switching Taft Robinson to quarterback. We'd like
your comment."

"Switching shit," he said.

"It's the truth, Hobbsie," I said. "Coach is going over to
a whole new offense just for the Centrex game. He wants
a quarterback who can run. Sprint-outs, roll-outs, options,
bootlegs. You see, he wants a quarterback who can
run."

"I'm the quarterback."

"It's just for one game."

"I'm the quarterback."

"But you can't run, Hobbsie. He wants a quarterback
who can run."

"We're undefeated in three games," Hobbs said. "I've
got sixty-two percent completions. I've been intercepted
just once and that's because Jessup broke the pattern and

he'll tell you that himself. I've been concentrating. I've been taking command in the huddle. I've been reading the blitz just like Coach taught me."

"But you can't run."

"I can throw, damn it. Can he throw?"

"Sure he can throw. He can do anything. You know that as well as I do. Coach thinks with Taft at quarterback we'll be able to do a lot more with our offense. It's a total offense concept. It's a reordering of priorities."

"I don't understand it. We've been doing real well up to now."

"We've been playing leprosariums and barbers' colleges. Coach wants something special to spring on Centrex."

"He's putting you on," Buddy Shock said.

"Is that right, Gary?"

"That's right," I said.

"You son of a bitch," Hobbs said.

Vern Feck ran around blowing a whistle and each player reported to his respective coach. The six running backs formed a circle around Oscar Veech. He was trying to think of something to say. Finally he focused on me.

"Button up when you get hit, Harkness. You haven't been buttoning up. You lost the ball once against those people and you almost lost it two other times."

"I was running with reckless abandon."

"Run with reckless abandon until you're hit. When you're hit, button up."

"Right."

"Button up. Become fetal. Hug that ball. Hug it. Hug it."

"Yes sir."

"Lee Roy, what am I talking about, Lee Roy?"

"I wasn't listening, sir," Lee Roy Tyler said.

"Typical," Veech said. "That's typical of the whole attitude around here. You people are a bunch of feeble-minded shit farmers. You're lazy, you're self-satisfied, you're stupid. In my considered opinion, you're a bunch of feebs. If you can't concentrate, you can't play football for this team. Awright now. What was I talking about, Hopper?"

"Buttoning up."

"Lee Roy, what are you supposed to do when your quarterback calls trips right and you're parked out there in the slot ready to fly and suddenly it dawns on you that they're in a zone? What do you do, Lee Roy?"

"Sir?"

"Lee Roy, you're a dung beetle. Shit is your proper environment. You do nothing, that's what you do. You run your damn pattern."

"Yes sir."

"Let's get real basic here. Deering, who do you take out on a weak-side sweep against a four-three?"

"Sir, I take out the linebacker."

"You take out the end, feeb. Your wide receiver cracks back on the linebacker."

"It's coming back to me now," Jim Deering said.

"If you had half a brain you'd be dangerous," Veech said. "Come on, let's get out of here before I hemorrhage."

We went over for a joint conference with Tom Cook Clark and his three quarterbacks, Garland Hobbs, Terry Madden and Byrd Whiteside. Then Vern Feck brought his linebackers over and we got Randy King to center for us so we could practice defending against the blitz, two setbacks and the center against blitz variations by the three linebackers. It was a timing drill really; we were wearing pads and headgear but there wasn't supposed to be any real contact. Madden was at quarterback. Bobby Hopper and I were behind him. On the first snapback, Champ Conway slipped and fell before he even reached me. Vern Feck was all over him in a second.

"Shitbird!" he screamed. "Shit, shit, shitbird. You got dumb feet, Conway. Messages from your brain must get clogged up somewhere around your kneecap. We got people ready to take your place, shitbird. Now you remember that."

"Audibilize," Tom Cook Clark was saying to Madden. "When you see them leaning like that, get ready to audibilize."

"Awright, awright, awright," Oscar Veech shouted, clapping his hands for no apparent reason.

"What are you, Conway?"

"Shitbird, sir."

Later a fight broke out between Randy King and a reserve linebacker, John Butler. King got Butler in a headlock and tried to spin him quickly to the ground. He ended his spin holding Butler's helmet. He caught a forearm from behind, then got spun around himself and kicked in the leg. He went down, grunting, and Butler jumped on him and they wrestled for a while, making dust. King, on the bottom, tried to pull Butler's jersey over his head. Finally the coaches stopped it and we got going again. Several plays later the blocking got sloppy, and Hobbs, at quarterback now, ran out of the pocket a bit prematurely. A whistle blew, rather softly, as if reluctant to call attention to itself, and we watched Creed come walking across the field. Hobbs put his hands on his hips and looked at the grass. Creed, taking his time, began speaking while he was still ten yards away, very quietly though, with forbearance.

"You've got to stay in the pocket, son."

"Yes sir, I know."

"You bailed out too early. You've got to stand firm even with all that meat coming in at you. If you can't do that, you can't play for me. Now that's a fact."

"Yes sir."

"Gary, that blocking was dreadful."

"Yes sir," I said.

King and Butler were fighting again. Creed heard the noise and turned slowly to watch. Since both of them wore linemen's facemasks, it was extremely difficult to draw blood, the unannounced purpose and only real satisfaction of such a fight. So they started kicking and wrestling again, pulling at each other's equipment, not tactically but in frustration, the pads, the faceguard, the helmet itself. King down now, John Butler kicked him in the stomach. Somebody pushed Butler away. King was through for the afternoon. They had to help him off. Butler stood alone near the sideline. Creed walked slowly across the field toward the offensive linemen, who were running wind sprints. I watched Bloomberg for a moment. Then we went back to our blitz drill. Everybody ignored Butler. He stood off to one side, watching. Five minutes later (you could feel it), we forgave him.

Sam Trammel, who coached the receivers, called the starting offensive and defensive units together for a dummy scrimmage. Vern Feck jumped in and out of the defensive huddle, checking on his boys, little pink face half-shady under the baseball cap, whistle bouncing off his wet T-shirt. I went through the motions; the motions seemed to reciprocate. I blocked, I carried the ball, I ran pass patterns. Out on a deep pattern I watched the ball spiral toward me, nose dropping now, laces spinning, my hands up and fingers spread, eyes following the ball right into my hands, here, now, and then lengthening my stride, breaking toward the middle, seeing myself on large-screen color TV as I veered into the end zone. The afternoon went by in theoretically measured stages, gliding, and I moved about not as myself but as some sequence from the idea of motion, a brief arrangement of schemes and physical laws abstracted from the whole. Everything was wonderfully automatic, in harmony, dreamed by genius. Cruising over the middle on a circle pattern, just loafing because the play was directed elsewhere, I got blasted for no reason by the free safety, Lenny Wells. I rolled over twice, enjoying the grass, and then got to my feet and patted Lenny on the rump.

"How to hit, baby," I told him.

It ended as it had begun, two laps around the goal

posts. On the first turn a tackle named Ted Joost, who was Randy King's roommate, bumped John Butler right into the goal post and kept on going. Butler ran after him and jumped on his back. Joost shook him off and they started swinging. I jogged past them and by the time I made the far turn and headed back it was all over. I walked toward Staley Hall with Bing Jackmin.

"I can't take much more of this," he said.

"Of what?"

"The antiquated procedures."

"What do you mean?" I said.

"All the procedures around here are antiquated. Blocking sleds are antiquated whether you know it or not. Agility drills are antiquated. We even have to bend down and touch our toes. Gary, this is the second half of the twentieth century. That stuff went out with the gladiators. We're using antiquated procedures and we don't even know it."

"You said yourself that we hark back. We hark back, you said. You're the one who coined that dumb phrase referring to the connection between then and now."

"Hyperatavistic," he said.

"I don't think that was it."

"Whatever it was, I still think football is antiquated. And you want to know what else it is? I've already given you a hint."

"What else, Bing?"

"It's gladiatorial," he said. "They fatten us up and then put us in the arena together. They train us to kill, more or less."

"Lead a revolt," I said.

"Coach would break me in half."

Howard Lowry was walking ahead of us. Howard was known as Boxcar. He was a starting tackle on defense and one of the few men on the squad who had normal human flab around his middle. He went about 265, packed low and very wide, and he was considered immovable.

Howard roomed with Billy Mast, a reserve back on defense. Billy was in the process of memorizing Rilke's ninth Duino Elegy in German, a language he did not understand. It was for a course he was taking in the untellable.

13

MYNA CORBETT AND THE responsibilities of beauty were to occupy me on and off for the rest of the year. I don't know exactly what it was I felt for her, or thought about her, or expected to give or receive. There are a thousand kinds of love. The simplest thing to say is that she made me feel comfortable. She created a private balance of nature, a sense of things being right, or almost right, both in themselves and against a larger requirement. So this love in a way was ecological; she made me feel at peace with my environment and maybe on my better days I did the same for her. Since my examinations of life sometimes ended in oblique forms of self-mockery, and since my investigative projects often manifested themselves as parodies of hunger or grief or exile, it was refreshing to seek in this woman a perfect circle whose reality overpowered the examiner's talent for reducing in size and meaning whatever variety of experience he was currently engaged in sampling.

Myna owned half a million dollars and membership in a science-fiction book club. There, by most standards, her attraction ended. She weighed about 165 pounds. Her face had several blotches of varying size and her hair hung in limp tangled clusters. She bit her nails, she waddled, she never shut up. We had two classes together,

Mexican geography and a sort of introduction to exobiology. Myna was the only female in the geography class (traditionally a course for football players) and seemed quite serious about the layout of Mexico. We got along well from the very beginning. I enjoyed listening to her talk and I liked the total liberty of her clothing. There was a sense of cavalcade to the way she dressed. Any number of fashion eras were likely to be represented at a given time. The feeling was warm, color-abundant, distinctly antihistorical.

We had mock picnics behind the Quonset hut—chopped almonds and Gatorade. Myna would usually bring along a science-fiction novel. She'd eat and read simultaneously, bouncing slightly on the brown grass when she reached a particularly invigorating passage. It was during our third or fourth picnic, on an unseasonably cool day, that we got involved for the first time in the responsibilities of beauty. Myna wore a carved plastic bracelet, meshed gold chains around her neck, and a hand-embroidered Victorian shawl over a silk gypsy blouse and floor-length patchwork skirt. Her boots were studded with blue stars.

"I've just realized what's really curious about you," I said. "Somehow you don't transmit any sense of a personal future."

"I'm a now person, Gary."

"That's good because I'm a then person."

"I know," she said. "That's why I like you. I need some perspective in my life."

"You'll hate me for saying this, Myna, but I think you're one of the prettiest girls I've ever known. Man or boy. Pound for pound."

"People are always telling me that. What a pretty face I have. It's just a thing you say to fat girls. It's supposed to make us guilty so we'll lose weight."

"But it's true," I said.

"I know it's true. All I have to do is lose fifty pounds and go to a skin doctor. But I like myself the way I am. I don't want to be beautiful or desirable. I don't have the strength for that. There are too many responsibilities. Things to live up to. I feel like I'm consistently myself. So many people have someone else stuck inside them. Like inside that big large body of yours there's a scrawny kid with thick glasses. Inside my father there's a vicious police dog, a fascist killer animal. Almost everybody has something stuck inside them. Inside me there's a sloppy emotional overweight girl. I'm the same, Gary, inside and out. It's hard to be beautiful. You have an obligation to people. You almost become public property. You can lose yourself and get almost mentally disturbed on just the public nature of being beautiful. Don't think I haven't thought about it. You can get completely lost in that whole dumb mess. And anyway who's to say what's beautiful and what's ugly?"

"There are standards."

"Whose?"

"I don't know. The Greeks. The Etruscans. You can't escape some things. History forces you to listen and to see."

"You have to balance history with science fiction," she said. "It's the only way to keep sane."

"We'll have another picnic tomorrow."

"Jesus, can we?"

"We can do anything we want, Myna."

"Can we bring something besides chopped almonds? Can we bring vegetable pancakes and maybe brownies?"

"We can bring anything we want as long as it's humble and meatless."

"Can we not bring this blanket? Can we bring a different blanket? I don't like this one. It makes me think of dead baby rabbits."

"It's been in my family for generations."

"The way you say some things. I actually believe you. I think you're serious. Then it hits me that something's not right. Can I bring my book again?"

"Of course."

"Can I wear my orange dress that you like so much?"

"You look like an explosion over the desert. Yes, you can wear it."

"Can I bring my tarot cards with me?"

"Of course you can. Absolutely. It's a picnic."

"Thank you, Gary."

14

MOST LIVES ARE GUIDED by clichés. They have a soothing effect on the mind and they express the kind of widely accepted sentiment that, when peeled back, is seen to be a denial of silence. Their menace is hidden with the darker crimes of thought and language. In the face of death, this menace vanishes altogether. Death is the best soil for cliché. The trite saying is never more comforting, more restful, as in times of mourning. Flowers are set about the room; we stand very close to walls, uttering the lush banalities.

Norgene Azamanian's name did not seem ridiculous for long. We knew that nothing is too absurd to happen in America. Norgene, the man and the name, soon became ordinary, no less plausible than refrigerators or bibles or the names for these objects. When he died, of injuries sustained in an automobile accident, we repeated certain phrases to each other and dedicated our next game to his memory. A local minister called him a fallen warrior. An article in the school paper quoted the president, Mrs. Tom Wade, as saying that his untimely death at the age of twenty-one would serve as a tragic reminder that our destiny is in the hands of a Being or Force dwelling beyond the scope of man's reason. Norgene wasn't a very good football player. But death had overwhelmed even his mediocrity and we conspired with his passing to make him gigantic. For many of us it was a first experience with death. We believed the phrases. He was indeed a fallen warrior; we were unquestionably reminded of our destinies. We took the field on the night of Norgene's memorial game and played like magnificent young gods, not out to avenge death but only to honor the dead, to remake memory as a work of art. That was the first half. In the second half the whole game fell apart. There were fights, broken plays, every kind of penalty. We still won easily. But the last hour left a bad taste (as the saying goes) in everyone's mouth.

Several weeks later, sometime between three and six in the morning, Tom Cook Clark shot himself in the head with an ivory-handled Colt .45. Emmett Creed referred to him in a eulogy as one of the best football minds in the country. He was also a molder of young men and a fine interdenominational example of all those fortunate enough to have been associated with him. Creed himself assumed the deceased man's responsibilities with the quarterbacks. The wake was held at the funeral home in town because there was nowhere in particular to send the body and no family to send it to. Everyone commented on how good the embalmed corpse looked. This became the theme of the wake. We assembled in the anteroom, clinging to walls, avoiding the center of the room for some reason, and we told each other how good the dead man looked, as if he were not dead at all but only waxed and well-dressed as part of some process of rejuvenation and would soon be buzzed awake, thinner than ever and quite refreshed. We reacted to the impact of death in this way, exchanging comical remarks in all seriousness, consoling each other with handshakes and slogans. Major Staley came to pay his respects. The major commanded the Air Force ROTC unit at the school. He saw me and came over. We shook hands, slowly and delicately, foregoing on this special occasion all intimations of virility.

"I understand he was despondent because of ill health," the major said.

We heard about the collision right away. It happened only about a quarter of a mile from campus. It was about ten at night. State troopers stood on the road, writing in their little books, copying from each other. They indentified Norgene from the contents of his wallet. There were three others dead, one a girl (passenger, female, white). Her legs stuck out of the wreck, terribly white, the only white things in all that blood and swirling red light, the only things quiet in the voices and noise. I wondered who she was. I also wondered why her death seemed more wasteful than the others. I kept looking at her legs. Then I went back to my room, thinking about the extra syllable in the fallen warrior's Christian name, how it had shamed tradition and brought bad luck.

This was Major Staley's first year here. His father was the school's most famous alumnus, a three-letter man and a war hero, one of the crew on the Nagasaki mission. The major was about thirty-eight years old. He taught just one course, Aspects of Modern War. Since I wasn't part of the cadet wing I had taken to seating myself in the last row, a bit of civilian humility. One day I asked the major how many megatons would have to be contained in the warhead of an antimissile missile in order to guarantee interception of an SS-9 missile with multiple warheads.

"You'd probably need in excess of a two-meg warhead to get the kind of x-ray pulse-intensity you're talking about."

I was fascinated by the way the state troopers copied from each other's little books. One trooper stood writing, another at his shoulder writing what the first one wrote. They checked each other out until it was apparent that they had reached an accord. It was a safeguard against errors and stray facts. There couldn't possibly be a mistake if they all had the same information.

In my room that night, before falling asleep, I tried to imagine where Tom Cook Clark came from, what he thought, what kind of life he led. I don't know what made me think of him that particular night. (At that point, of course, he was still alive.) I tried to understand who he was and what made him whoever he was when he seemed no more than a face, a hat, a certain way of talking. He existed (then). I lay in bed thinking of him as I had thought of only several others in my entire life, all casual acquaintances, blanks more or less. I could guess nothing about him. I could imagine nothing. I could invent nothing. Why did he remain so blank? It made me feel stupid and weak. Perhaps the man had a need to live in another man's mind. His existence might be threatened if he could not be brought to life in perhaps the only mind that had ever tried to reconstruct him. It was strange that he would kill himself in a matter of weeks. Maybe the failure was mine, the ill health mine, that blank life a kind of notebook in need of somebody else's facts, those facts a mass of jargon for the military mind, this jargon resembling clichés passed from mourner to mourner in the form of copied notes. But it was just another of my philosophic speculations, to think his life depended on what my mind could make of him, existence turning on a wheel, numerical, nonbuddhist, the notes comforting the notebook, numbers covering the words used to cover silence. He was a scholarly man, I thought (in the anteroom of the funeral home), remembering that he smoked a pipe and did not use profanity.

"Given three warheads per missile and an accuracy factor of a quarter mile, they'd need four to five hundred of the SS-nine classification to achieve first-strike destruction capability of ninety-five percent relative to what we could hit back with in terms of Minuteman counter capacity," the major added.

Billy Mast, who roomed two doors away from me, worked every night at memorizing a long poem in a language he'd never read before, never spoken, never even heard except in one or two movies. Billy got extremely high marks in everything. Scholastically he ranked in the ninety-ninth percentile. In several of his classes, prorated scoring systems were devised according to the standards he set. Every night he did more work on the elegy. I'd visit him sometimes just to hear the sounds he made, his guttural struggle against those grudging consonants. He liked to hit his desk with both hands as he recited. Billy's course in the untellable was restricted to ten students. Knowledge of German was a prerequisite for being refused admission.

Closing my eyes, finally, on the night of the accident, I wanted to dream that I put my hand between the dead girl's legs. Arousals of guilt had considerable appeal to me, particularly on waking. I liked to lie in bed, viewing after-images of morbid sex and trying to apportion guilt between the conscious mind and the unconscious. But that night's sleep turned out to be a restless one, empty of remembered dreams.

15

"WHO WAS THE GREATER MAN?" Bloomberg said. "You get just one try. Sir Francis Drake or the prophet Isaiah? Take your time answering. It's not as obvious as it seems."

"How can you compare them?" Andy Chudko said. "They were in two different fields."

"The answer seems obvious only at first. Be very careful."

"I don't think it seems obvious at all," Chudko said.

I stood in the doorway. Bloomberg and Andy Chudko occupied the beds. Anatole was supine, two pillows beneath his head, hands folded on his chest. Chudko sat on my bed, facing the doorway, his right foot (extended to infinity) at a 45-degree angle to the door (when closed). I noted other angles, elevations, intervals, and then situated myself carefully on the chair by the window, between the beds, facing past both men toward the open doorway, toward the corridor or trade route. Chudko's head and torso met without benefit of a neck. His whole body in fact seemed welded, part joined to part in bursts of heat and pressure. His silver guitar was on the other chair, the chair by the door.

"I don't understand you, Bloomers. Gary, you room with this guy. What do you make of him?"

"Our next secretary of defense."

"My roommate will be glad to hear that I'm off my diet as of an hour ago. I think he'll rejoice in that."

"I do. I definitely approve."

"I've seen my mistake," Bloomberg said. "I thought I would become more efficient if I ate less. I thought the discipline of dieting would be good for me. It would make me quicker in body and therefore quicker in mind. It would give me a sense of physical definition and therefore of spiritual awareness. This was all wrong. I thought I would feel better if I weighed less. I thought I would have more respect for myself. I thought I'd gain in self-assurance and in the general loftiness of my ideals. None of this happened. It was all part of the Jewish thing, you see. I thought the self-control of dieting would lead to the self-control needed to unjew myself. But it didn't work out that way. As I lost weight, as I continued to struggle against food and its temptations, I began to lose the idea of myself. I was losing the idea of my body, who it belonged to, what exactly it was, where all the different parts of it were located, what it looked like from different angles and during the various times of the day and evening. I was losing the most important part of my being.

Obesity. What I had considered self-control was really self-indulgence. To make me pretty. To give me quick feet. I realize now that these things aren't important, that they're nothing compared with my individual reality. I dropped to two-ninety, then to two eighty-two. My self-awareness started to fade. It was a terrible shedding of the skin. I was losing more and more of myself. I was losing more of the old body and more of the newly acquired mind. If this disappearance were to continue, I would soon be left with only one thing. Gentlemen, I allude to my Jewishness. This is the subsoil, as it were, of my being. It would be the only thing left and I would be, in effect, a fourteen-year-old Jewish boy once more. Would I start telling silly jokes about my mother? Would I put some of that old ghetto rhythm in my voice—jazz it up a little? Would the great smelly guilt descend on me? I don't want to hear a word about the value of one's heritage. I am a twentieth-century individual. I am working myself up to a point where I can exist beyond guilt, beyond blood, beyond the ridiculous past. Thank goodness for America. In this country there's a chance to accomplish such a thing. I want to look straight ahead. I want to see things clearly. I'd like to become single-minded and straightforward in the most literal sense of those words. History is no more accurate than prophecy. I reject the wrathful God of the Hebrews. I reject the Christian God of love and money, although I don't reject love itself or money itself. I reject heritage, background, tradition and birthright. These things merely slow the progress of the human race. They result in war and insanity, war and insanity, war and insanity."

I got up and closed the door. Then I returned to the chair by the window. I turned it around and sat with my arms over the back of the chair. I faced the closed door. Bloomberg raised his right arm, maintaining that position—body supine, one arm bent across his chest, second arm in the air—for the length of the ensuing narration. He appeared mad, an imprisoned prophet or a figure in a very old painting, a man about to die, his last word spoken to a finger tip of light.

"As the world's ranking authority on environmental biomedicine, I have been asked to lend the weight of my opinion to yet another tense seminar on the future of the earth. My friends, there is nothing to fear. Soon we'll harvest the seas, colonize the planets, control every aspect of the weather. We'll develop nuclear reactors to provide the English-speaking world with unlimited energy, safely and cheaply. Our radio astronomers will communicate with beings at the very ends of the universe. We'll build hydraulic robots to make automation obsolete. We'll manufacture plastic lungs and brains. We'll reprogram human cells with new genetic information to wipe out inherited disease. Obsolescence itself will become obsolete. We'll recycle everything. Shoes to food. Candles to paper. Rocks to light bulbs. The philosophical question has been asked: what will become of death? Gentlemen, I have the answer right here. The sealed envelope please."

Andy Chudko looked at me. He got up, took the guitar from the chair by the door and then opened the door and left, closing it behind him. Bloomberg began to speak again. I was sorry Chudko hadn't left the guitar. In some obscure way, its presence would have been a comfort.

16

THE MOTEL WAS about two miles from campus. I walked out there along the edge of the road. Fragments of glass flared in the sun. I passed a number of dead animals, just scraps of fur now, small pieces of flesh completely mac-

adamized, part of the highway. Finally I reached the motel. It was a gray building, barely distinguishable from the
land around it. Major Staley had been staying there since
the school year began. I didn't know what kind of car the
major drove so I went into the office and got his room
number from an old woman half-asleep over a bowl of
Shredded Wheat. The major had a towel in his hands
when he came to the door. He was wearing his uniform
trousers and shirt, the shirt unbuttoned and outside the
pants, sleeves rolled up around the forearms. Some blue
ROTC manuals were stacked on a table. Above the bed
was a three-dimensional picture of mountains.

"Wife and kids are still up in Colorado. I sure as hell
miss them. I hope to have them down here real soon now.
Our house should be ready in ten days. I've lived in more
places than a stray cat."

"There's a kind of theology at work here. The bombs
are a kind of god. As his power grows, our fear naturally
increases. I get as apprehensive as anyone else, maybe
more so. We have too many bombs. They have too many
bombs. There's a kind of theology of fear that comes out
of this. We begin to capitulate to the overwhelming
presence. It's so powerful. It dwarfs us so much. We say
let the god have his way. He's so much more powerful
than we are. Let it happen, whatever he ordains. It used
to be that the gods punished men by using the forces of
nature against them or by arousing them to take up their
weapons and destroy each other. Now god is the force of
nature itself, the fusion of tritium and deuterium. Now
he's the weapon. So maybe this time we went too far in
creating a being of omnipotent power. All this hardware.
Fantastic stockpiles of hardware. The big danger is that
we'll surrender to a sense of inevitability and start flinging
mud all over the planet."

"We're talking about a one-megaton device. All right,
you're standing nine miles from ground zero. If it's a clear

day, you get second-degree burns. Guaranteed. One hundred megs, you may as well forget it. If you were seventy-five miles out, you'd still get second-degree. Depending on the variables, your house might even ignite. That's just the first flash. After that comes the firestorm, like Tokyo, like Hamburg, like Dresden, like Hiroshima. Structurally the older cities in the U.S. are very susceptible to firestorms. Building density is high and combustible material per building is high. Tucson might escape a firestorm. New York, Baltimore, Boston—forget it. Nagasaki didn't get too much burn. They had a low density and the wind was blowing right. Hamburg was something else. Hamburg was a hot place to be. Over a thousand degrees Fahrenheit if you can imagine what that's like. They found bodies naked except for shoes. That was heat that did that, not fire. Heat disintegrated the clothes. They found bodies shrunken, dry as paper. That was the intense heat. The other thing in a firestorm is carbon monoxide."

"I've had a checkered career at best."

"I think what'll happen in the not-too-distant future is that we'll have humane wars. Each side agrees to use clean bombs. And each side agrees to limit the amount of megatons he uses. In other words we'll get together with them beforehand and there'll be an agreement that if the issue can't be settled, whatever the issue might be, then let's make certain we keep our war as relatively humane as possible. So we agree to use clean stuff. And we actually specify the number of megatons; let's just say hypothetically one thousand megs for each side. So then what we've got is a two-thousand-megaton war. We might go further and say we'll leave your cities alone if you leave ours alone. We make it strictly counterforce. So right off the bat you avoid the fallout hazard and millions of bonus kills, or deaths from fallout. And at the same time you eliminate city-trading and punishing strikes

against the general population. Of course the humanistic
mind crumbles at the whole idea. It's the most hideous
thing in the world to these people that such ideas even
have to be mentioned. But the thing won't go away. The
thing is here and you have to face it. The prospect of a
humane war may be hideous and all the other names you
can think of, but it's still a prospect. And as an alternative
to all the other things that could happen in the event of
war, it's relatively acceptable. My fellow co-liberals are
always the first to jump all over me when I talk about
something like humane warfare. But the thing has to be
considered. People close their minds. They think nuclear
war has to be insensate, both sides pushing all the buttons
and the whole thing is over in two hours. In reality it's
likely to be very deliberate, very cautious, a kind of thing
that's almost fought in slow motion. And the limited humane variant is the most acceptable. Negotiations could
easily take that turn. A war may have to be fought; it may
be unavoidable in terms of national pride or to avoid
blackmail or for a number of other reasons. And negotiations, whatever remains of negotiations, whatever talking
is still going on, this could easily lead both countries to
the humane war idea as the least damaging kind of thing
in the face of all the variants. So they hit our military and
industrial targets with any number of bombs and missiles
totaling one thousand megatons and we do the same to
them. There'd be all sorts of controls. You'd practically
have a referee and a timekeeper. Then it would be over
and you'd make your damage assessment. The sensing
devices go to work. The magnetic memory drums are
tapped. The computers figure out damage and number of
casualties. Recovery time is estimated. We wouldn't be
the same strong industrial society after one thousand megs
but our cities would still be standing and the mortality
rate would be in the fairly low percentiles, about eight to
twelve percent. With no fallout in the atmosphere, or a
relatively minimum amount, we'd have no problems with

environmental stress, with things like temperature changes, erosion, droughts, insect devastation, and we'd avoid the radiation diseases by and large, the infections, the genetic damage. So we'd get going again relatively soon. It wouldn't be nearly as bad as most people might expect. On the other hand this entire concept is full of flaws."

"Nagasaki was an embarrassment to the art of war."

"The nuclear nations have a stockpile of fissionable material I would estimate in the neighborhood of sixty thousand megatons in terms of explosive power. That's a personal estimate, based on whatever tech-data I've been able to accumulate in the journals and bulletins, accurate within a factor of maybe three or four. But just for the heck of it, figure that out in terms of pounds of TNT. That's pounds now, not tons. I bet you can't do it without paper and pencil. The trick is to keep count of the zeros."

"War is the ultimate realization of modern technology. For centuries men have tested themselves in war. War was the final test, the great experience, the privilege, the honor, the self-sacrifice or what have you, the absolutely ultimate determination of what kind of man you were. War was the great challenge and the great evaluator. It told you how much you were worth. But it's different today. Few men want to go off and fight. We prove ourselves, our manhood, in other ways, in making money, in skydiving, in hunting mountain lions with bow and arrow, in acquiring power of one kind or another. And I think we can forget ideology. People invent that problem, at least as far as the U.S. is concerned. It has no real bearing as far as we're concerned. Obviously we can live with Communism; we've been doing it long enough. So people invent that. That's the grotesque sense of patriotism at work in this country. Today we can say that war is a test of opposing technologies. We can say this more than ever because it's more true than it ever was. Look, what would our cartoonists do if they wanted to satirize the Chinese, if we were in a period of extreme tension with the Chinese and the editorial cartoonists wanted to stir up a little patriotism? Would they draw slanted eyes and pigtails the way they drew buck teeth for the Japanese in the forties? No, no, they wouldn't make fun of the people at all. They'd satirize the machines, the nuclear capability, the weapons and such of the Chinese. They'd draw firecrackers and kites. War has always told men what they were capable of under stress. Now it informs the machines. It's the best test of a country's technological skills. Are all your gaseous diffusion plants going at top efficiency? Are your ICBM guidance and control mechanisms ready to work perfectly? You get the answers when war breaks out. Your technology doesn't know how good it is until it goes to war, until it's been tested in the ultimate way. I don't think we care too much about individual bravery anymore. It's better to be efficient than brave. So that's it then. It's regrettable but there it is. And your technology isn't any good if it can't beat the enemy's. Your weapons have to be more efficient than theirs, more reliable, more accurate, more deadly. Your technology has to reach peak efficiency. It has to stretch itself out, over-reach itself; it has to improve itself almost instantaneously. It won't do this without the stress of war. War brings out the best in technology."

"Major, there's no way to express thirty million dead. No words. So certain men are recruited to reinvent the language."

"I don't make up the words, Gary."

"They don't explain, they don't clarify, they don't express. They're painkillers. Everything becomes abstract. I admit it's fascinating in a way. I also admit the problem goes deeper than just saying some crypto-Goebbels in the Pentagon is distorting the language."

"Somebody has to get it before the public regardless of language. It has to be aired in public debate, clinically, the whole thing, no punches pulled, no matter how terrible the subject is and regardless of language. It has to be discussed."

"I don't necessarily disagree."

"Look, Gary, if I go out and talk to different groups about this sort of thing, it doesn't make me some kind of monster who likes to expound or whatever the word is on the consequences of nuclear exchange, who likes to stand up there before a group and talk about mass death and all the rest of it. If I try to inform people so they'll do something about the situation, the gravity of it, then I'm performing a service, or at least it seems to me. I'm not some kind of monstrous creature who enjoys talking about the spectacle of megadeath, the unprecedented scale of this kind of thing. It has to be talked about and expounded on. It has to be described for people, clinically and graphically, so they'll know just what it is they're facing."

"I don't necessarily disagree, major."

"The greatest thrill of my life was getting a ride in the XB-seventy. That was the greatest thrill of my life."

"Weapons technology is so specialized that nobody has to feel any guilt. Responsibility is distributed too thinly for that. It's the old warriors like myself who have to take the blame for what the so-called technocrats and multidimensional men are up to."

"What did you want to see me about exactly?"
"Just nuclear war, sir. What it might be like."

"First to sixth hour after detonation the ground-zero circle is drenched with fallout. By the end of the first day the dose-rate begins to slow down. After a few months it slows down considerably. It all depends on the megatons, the fission yield, air or surface burst, wind velocity, mean pressure altitude, descent time, median particle size."

"Ten megatons of fission produce one million curies of strontium ninety. What does that do to milk calcium levels? There's a factor-four discrimination against strontium in the human body. Newly forming bone attains a level eight times greater than the level that's acceptable. Then there's cerium one forty-four, plutonium two thirty-nine, barium one-forty. What else have we got? Zinc sixty-five in fish. Also radioiodine. That's milk, children, thyroid cancer."

"The average lethal mutation in an autosome persists for twenty-two generations."

"The aging process, the natural aging process means there's a slowdown in cell turnover, cellular turnover. Now you get a cell population exposed to a particular radiation dose and what you have is an aggravation of the slowdown thing, the radiation on top of the natural degenerative body process. The average life span undergoes a decrease. If you're exposed to three-hundred-R whole-body radiation, say within seven days of when the thing hits, and then say another hundred R over the entire first year, you lose about eleven years, you undergo a life-span reduction of eleven years. Sublethal doses also cause reproduction problems. There are problems with microcephalic offspring. There are abnormal terminations and stillbirths. There's a problem with inferior skeletal maturation of male and female progeny. There is formation of abnormal lens tissue in offspring. There are chromosome breaks. There is sterility of course. There is general reduction of body size of male offspring six years of age and under. However, the Japanese data indicates that congenital malformation frequency would not necessarily vary from the norm as far as the first post-bomb generation is concerned."

"The rate is six per thousand per one hundred R. That's twenty-four hundred lethal genetic events per four hundred thousand people exposed to one hundred roentgens. Hiroshima supports this formula."

The sun. The desert. The sky. The silence. The flat stones. The insects. The wind and the clouds. The moon. The stars. The west and east. The song, the color, the smell of the earth.

I headed back to campus through the desert. The sun was low, swept by slowly moving clouds in its decline, a crust of moon also visible, more pure in silence than the setting sun. I walked quickly, the only moving thing. Nothing else stirred, not even waning light folding over stone and not the slightest flick of an insect at the perimeter of vision. The sound of my feet was the only sound, my body all there was of moving parts. I counted cadence for a few beats in a pleasantly regimental voice, nonchalant and southern. The wind was light and dry. The plants did not move in the wind. I remembered the black stone, the stone painted black. I wondered if I'd be able to find it. It was important at that moment to come upon something that could be defined in one sense only, something not probable or variable, a thing unalterably itself. I ruled out the stone, too rich in enigma. I began counting cadence again. I managed the southern accent fairly well. I had a talent for accents, although I didn't make use of it very often because it seemed too easy a way to get people to laugh. I marched a bit longer. Then I saw something that terrified me. I stood absolutely still, as if motion might impede my understanding of this moment. It was three yards in front of me, excrement, a low mound of it, simple shit, nothing more, yet strange and vile in this wilderness, perhaps the one thing that did not betray its definition. I tried not to look any longer. I held my

breath, fearing whatever smell might still be clinging to
that spot. I wanted my senses to deny this experience,
leaving it for wind and dust. There was the graven art of
a curse in that sight. It was overwhelming, a terminal act,
nullity in the very word, shit, as of dogs squatting near
partly eaten bodies, rot repeating itself; defecation, as of
old women in nursing homes fouling their beds; feces, as
of specimen, sample, analysis, diagnosis, bleak assess-
ments of disease in the bowels; dung, as of dry straw
erupting with microscopic eggs; excrement, as of final
matter voided, the chemical stink of self discontinued;
offal, as of butchered animals' intestines slick with shit
and blood; shit everywhere, shit in life cycle, shit as earth
as food as shit, wise men sitting impassively in shit, armies retreating in that stench, shit as history, holy men
praying to shit, scientists tasting it, volumes to be com-
piled on color and texture and scent, shit's infinite treach-
ery, everywhere this whisper of inexistence. I hurried
toward campus. All around me the day was ending. I
crossed the highway and walked along the side of the
road. There was a car in the distance, coming toward me.
The wind picked up briefly. The low clouds moved across
the horizon. In time the college's buildings would come
into view. I looked down at the road as I walked. The
wind picked up again. I thought of men embedded in the
ground, all killed, billions, flesh cauterized into the earth,
bits of bone and hair and nails, man-planet, a fresh
intelligence revolving through the system. Once again I
rebuked myself for misspent reflections. I could hear the
car now, just barely, a small murderous hum, as of
unnamed sounds at the end of a hall. Perhaps there is no
silence. Or maybe it's just that time is too compact to
allow for silence to be felt. But in some form of void,
freed from consciousness, the mind remakes itself. What
we must know must be learned from blanked-out pages.
To begin to reword the overflowing world. To subtract
and disjoin. To re-recite the alphabet. To make elemental
lists. To call something by its name and need no other

sound. I looked up. The car passed me, an army staff vehicle with a large circular antenna. Soon the campus lights were visible and I stopped for a few seconds, watching the day burn out.

The sun. The desert. The sky. The silence. The flat stones. The insects. The wind and the clouds. The moon. The stars. The west and east. The song, the color, the smell of the earth.

Blast area. Fire area. Body-burn area.

17

MYNA CORBETT SAT next to me in our exobiology class. The instructor was a little man named Alan Zapalac, who liked to be called Zap. He was about five feet four inches tall, not much older than the rest of us, and very mobile in his teaching methods. He had a distinctly limited stride, moving back and forth across the front of the room as he spoke, sometimes stalking the aisles. He spoke quickly, flowing over his own words, laughing almost in embarrassment when he said something he knew was quite perceptive. He waved his arms a lot and smiled maniacally at our more ridiculous statements. Every so often he sat on top of his desk or on the windowsill, his small feet pedaling the air.

"Formic acid trickles through the great halls of the universe. Way out there the thing is evolving, has evolved, is about to evolve, whatever synthesis you can guess at, methane, ammonia, hydrogen, water vapor, all acted on by present or unknown forms of energy to form amino acids which in turn are developed into proteins which in turn are acted on by nucleic acids to give us life in neon lettering across the sky, what harmony, what religion. Dextrorotation, think of it. I look at your faces and see no sign that this word rings any kind of bell. Somebody give me a sign. The person making any kind of intelligible comment gets to clap the erasers after class. The real point is how to grasp it, how to get beyond pure formulations and discussions of isotope content and get into the mystery of it. Four point five billion years. Science is religion, did you know that? Consider what it is we're talking about. Earthly origins, meteorites dropping from the heavens, creation of the solar system. But in approaching each other to discuss this thing we have to get through all the barriers imposed by all the allied sciences and disciplines—that of multiple definitions, that of cross-references nobody's even begun to put in any coherent form, that of terminologies which are untranslatable, that of expensive duplications, that of inconsistencies in even the most sophisticated testing equipment, that of speed outrunning itself in terms of who in what discipline is developing unforeseen procedures which completely wipe out so-and-so in what other discipline. Let me tell you about my childhood in Oregon."

Myna had a few words with Zapalac after class and then we left with two friends of hers, sisters, Esther and Vera Chalk, and had a picnic behind the Quonset hut. Myna had made meatless and breadless organic sandwiches; one of the Chalk girls brought along raw carrots and celery tonic. The sisters complimented Myna on her funky crystal-beaded suede dress. Then the three of them talked about me as I lay on the blanket with my arms crossed over my eyes. They said nice things mostly, how well-built I was, how my nose was slightly off-line in a pleasant way. Esther lifted my arms off my face during the part about the nose; she wanted to confirm something. Then we ate lunch and listened to Myna read a short story about a solar system inhabited by oxycephalic crea-

END ZONE · 73

tures who give birth to their own mothers. When it was over, Vera Chalk poured her tonic into a plastic cup.

"Zapalac gives me goose bumps," she said.

"I just adore that little man," Esther said. "He conveys a real primitive-appeal type thing."

"Did you hear him on electron bombardment? I swear he made poetry out of it."

"I like his teeth," Myna said.

"They're real white," Esther said.

"It's not that so much. It's how small they are."

"Remember daddy's teeth?" Vera said.

"They were gruesome."

"They were horse teeth. Gaa. I have a shit fit just thinking about them. Gaa."

"They were gruesome beyond belief. They were the perfect teeth for someone like him."

"My father's teeth are okay," Myna said. "It's the rest of him."

"Raw carrots are good for the teeth," Esther said. "Most people think it's carrots for the eyesight, milk for the teeth. But it's dumb to subdivide things that way. Carrots nourish the body and all the extensions of the body. It's carrots for whole-body harmony."

"She's into carrots pretty heavy," Vera said.

"How you chew them's important. You sort of project your jaw outward and then chomp down hard. You're supposed to think of the numeral seventeen while you're chewing them. The numeral seventeen is a numeral of immortal life. Raw vegetables have a link-up with certain forms of numerology."

"I don't know how Zapalac's teeth could chew anything," Myna said. "They're so small and tiny. I picture him eating a lot of soup and a lot of strained foods."

"Tell them about daddy's thumbs," Vera said.

"Don't remind me please."

"Our daddy had these gross thumbs. They were huge. They were immense, Gary. And they were so ugly they'd make you physically sick just to look at them. But we used to sneak little looks anyway and we were always afraid he'd catch us."

"Then he'd bite you with his horse teeth," I said.

"Gaa."

"Talk about something else," Esther said.

"Remember his thumbnails? They were brownish yellow. They didn't have any pink at all. They were scab colored."

"Oh God please," Esther said.

"It was real scary being anywhere near those thumbs. They were horrible-looking things. And he liked to use his thumb to pick his nose."

"Oh please no."

"We're here to comfort each other," Myna said.

After the picnic I went to my room. Bloomberg, wearing shorts with little slits in them, was on his bed, turned to the wall, asleep. After a while I was called to the telephone. I assumed someone in my family had died. On the way to the phone I wondered who it might be, which death would cause me the most grief, whether it was an accident or natural, and whether I would have to go home for the funeral if it was just an uncle or aunt. Then I picked up the phone and heard my mother's voice.

"How's your laundry?" she said.

"Fine—how's yours?"

I wasn't particularly relieved that no one had died. When we were finished talking I returned to my room. Anatole was on his back. His body rose and fell through a tidal sleep. I spent the afternoon looking out the window. That evening we went down to a team meeting. Tweego and Hauptfuhrer yelled at us for our performance of two days before, our sixth game. We had won 27–10 but it had been our worst game by far. We lost the ball four times on fumbles. Bing Jackmin missed an extra point and three field goals. The defensive unit wasn't aggressive, giving up just ten points only because the opposition was so pathetic; we knew it wouldn't be much of a contest when we saw their quarterback wearing number 78. Garland Hobbs didn't show much either. He threw only long passes in the first quarter, as if a sustained drive was too much trouble, and he missed his first six and then got intercepted before Creed placed a hand on his shoulder and spoke softly into his face. All these thing we were reminded of as we sat in the long low stone room under Staley Hall. Coming up was Centrex, the game that would make or break the season. In six games we had scored 246 points and given up 41. It didn't mean a thing if we couldn't win the next one.

"You got five days to get ready," Hauptfuhrer said. "This isn't Snow White and the seven dwarfs you're facing this time. This is a bunch of head-hunters. They like to hit. They have definite sadistic tendencies. This isn't another humpty dumpty outfit. This is a squad that's big and mean. You people got a long way to go in meanness. You think you're mean but you're not mean. Centrex is mean. They're practically evil. They'll stomp all over you. It'll be men against boys. You better execute out there. And you better play mean. They're head-hunters. They like to humiliate people. That's their stock in trade. You better get ready for the worst."

"Let me tell you about their head coach," Tweego said. "I know Jade Kiley. I've known him for years. I know every wart on his hide. And he's mean."

"You better believe it."

"And his boys are mean."

"They're quite a contingent," Hauptfuhrer said. "They like to hit."

"A Jade Kiley team likes to hit. That's been his trademark down the years. I've known Jade Kiley I don't know how long. His teams have always liked to hit. Jade Kiley doesn't let you put on a uniform unless you like to hit. Jade Kiley teams are hitting teams."

"They like to humiliate people. They're quite a contingent."

"You got your work cut out for you," Tweego said. "You got five days to get ready. We can help you get ready but we can't play the damn game for you. We can take you right up to kickoff. Then you're on your own."

"They'll stomp blue shit out of you," Hauptfuhrer said.

Creed didn't make an appearance. As the season progressed he had become more remote. We saw him only at practice and at the games. He no longer had his meals with the squad. At practice he stayed up in the tower or sat alone in the last row of benches in the small grandstand section used during the baseball season. During the games he remained in one spot on the sidelines, right at the midfield stripe, letting his assistants make all the decisions and control the flow of players. He seemed to be losing weight and he moved slowly now, with a slight limp.

When the meeting ended Raymond Toon and I went up to his room to watch television. I wanted to look at the replay of a game between the Detroit Lions and the Minnesota Vikings. It was a little early but he turned on the set anyway and we watched a program composed of film clips of hurricanes, tornadoes and avalanches. It was one of the most fascinating things I had ever seen. Raymond, stretched out in his chair, nearly spanned the walls.

"What do you think?" he said. "Can we beat them?"

"I'm watching this."

"They'll be tough. We've had it too easy all year. It'll make them seem that much tougher. But I guess all we can do is go out there and do the best we can. The man upstairs decides these things."

"Who do you mean, Toony?"

"The man upstairs," he said. "It's up to him what happens. All we can do is use our talents to the best of our ability. We can run, we can block, we can tackle, we can kick the ball and catch the ball. If the man upstairs decides we don't deserve to win, then we won't win. Gary, I'm a substitute tackle. I've done all I can to earn first-string status. I play my heart out every time I get in there.

Maybe I'm not mean enough. That's a criticism that's been leveled at me more than once. I know I try my best. I go all out on every play. I give one hundred and ten percent just like Coach demanded of us back last summer. It's like the notion of valuation in the hard market, Gary. Practitioners link the measurement of earnings magnitude to the need for assessing the variability that's expressed in the multiplier rate. This way you avoid double-counting the risk allowance. But I can't crack the starting lineup. And if the man upstairs wants it that way, that's good enough for me. He has his reasons."

"What are they?"

"I wouldn't even try to guess, Gary. I just know they're good reasons. But they're probably beyond our scope."

"Toony, this shit about the man upstairs. Is the man upstairs supposed to be synonymous with God or what? Because either way it's an outmoded concept. It's a concept that's incredibly outmoded. It makes absolutely no theological sense."

"Don't try to get me in a discussion," he said.

John Jessup walked in then, Raymond's roommate. The game came on and we all watched it, marveling at the pros, how easily they did the things we stumbled over. In slow motion the game's violence became almost tender, a series of lovely and sensual assaults. The camera held on fallen men, on men about to be hit, on those who did the hitting. It was a loving relationship with just a trace of mockery; the camera lingered a bit too long, making poetic sport of the wounded. We laughed at the most acrobatic spills and the hardest tackles and at the meanness of some of it, the gang tackles and cheap shots. We laughed especially at the meanness. After about ten minutes Raymond turned down the sound so he could practice his sportscasting. Jessup leaped for the set and turned the sound back up.

"I've had enough broadcasting from your big dumb face."

"I have to practice," Raymond said.

"This goddamn set is not to be goddamn touched. Now I'm serious about that."

"It's my set, John."

"I don't care if it was a gift from your grandmother who knitted it herself."

"John, I've never hurt a man on purpose in my whole life."

"And you ain't tonight, shitfinger."

Jessup was standing in front of the set now, guarding it. Raymond began to ease himself from the chair. I moved my head in order to see what the Lions would do on fourth and one inside the Minnesota 5. The field-goal team came on and I reached over and grabbed Raymond's arm.

"Go easy," I said. "We've got a hard week ahead of us. You're both tense. It's the tension. I feel it. Coach feels it. We all feel it. We're all tense and knotted up. Let's save the combat for Saturday. It's bound to be a long hard week. Toony, shake the man's hand."

I was right about the kind of week it would be. We did everything wrong in practice and the coaches raged at us. I spent a lot of time with Myna. Nothing helped very much. Wednesday's practice was the worst of the year and when we were only slightly better the next day, Creed issued word that Friday's light workout would be canceled. He also called the team captains in and suggested we have a beer party that night, Thursday, no coaches, no females, no time limit. The throwing of the beer cans started half an hour after the party began. It went from there to fights, to mass vomiting, to singing and comradeship. A defensive end named Larry Nix kept punching a door until he busted through. A few people fell asleep in their chairs or on the floor. There was a pissing contest with about twenty entries trying not for distance but for altitude—a broom held by two men being the crossbar as it were, the broom raised in stages as contestants dropped out and others progressed. It was the most disgusting, ridiculous and adolescent night I had ever spent. The floor of the lounge was covered with beer, urine and ketchup, and we kept slipping and falling and then getting up and getting casually knocked down again by somebody passing by. Clothes were torn and there was blood to be seen on a few grinning faces. There were tag-team wrestling matches, push-up contests, mock bullfights, and other events harder to classify. A bunch of men jumping repeatedly in the air with their hands at their sides. Seven people in a circle spitting at each other's shoes. Lloyd Philpot Jr. ate nine hamburgers in twenty-five minutes. Link Brownlee chugged a bottle of ketchup. Jim Deering and his brother Chuck traded ten quick bolo punches to the midsection, apparently reviving a boyhood tradition. It was a horrible night. They took off Billy Mast's clothes and threw him out the front door. Somebody pushed Gus de Rochambeau and he skidded past me over the beer and piss and put his hand through a window. I took out my handkerchief and bandaged him. Then we sang one of the school songs, Gus and I, and I didn't know whether I was singing seriously or making fun of the song and in a very short while I didn't know whether I was singing at all or just listening to Gus sing. I thought I could hear my own voice but I wasn't sure and so I stood there with Gus, not wanting to leave if I was still singing, and I watched my teammates slip and fall into the beer and get up sick and laughing.

Since there was no workout scheduled for Friday, I thought it would be a good idea to end the week as it had begun, a picnic with Myna and the Chalk sisters. The cyclic redundancy might be beneficial. I needed a feeling of restfulness, of things content enough in themselves to begin again, and I thought the warm drawling chatter of an identical picnic might put me at ease. Myna was available and so was Esther Chalk. Vera had a class but we talked her out of it and assembled behind the Quonset hut. I lay on the blanket with my arms over my face.

"We could all live somewhere," Myna said. "I have all

this money that's in my name. We could go to Mexico. A friend of mine knows where to get good stuff in Mexico City. We could buy a Rolls-Royce and pick up some stuff in Mexico City and drive into the mountains."

"You have money?" Esther said. "Gary, she has money?"

"Half a million."

"Oil depletion," Myna said.

"Half a million dollars?"

"My father wanted to send me to Bryn Mawr. So I had this decision to make. Either I could lose all my excess weight and kill my blemishes with cobalt or whatever they use and go to Bryn Mawr and be a beautiful and charming young lady and risk being supermiserable because of the responsibilities of that kind of thing. Or I could come a little west to out here and be emotional and do what I want. They're both better than staying home and out here you don't get nagged by responsibilities like the responsibilities of beauty."

"What are you going to do with the money?" Vera said.

"Gary," Esther said, "what's she going to do with the money?"

"I don't know."

"She should keep it."

"She should do whatever she wants," Esther said.

"She should keep it," Vera said. "She should hold on to it."

"I don't know much about things English. But the idea of riding around in a Rolls-Royce sounds pretty neat. And it's her money."

"But she shouldn't just throw it away. She should do something positive with it. Maybe open a shop. I'm into handicrafts, Gary. We could think up something worthwhile."

"She can throw it away if she wants to. It's her money, Vera."

"Don't call me that. You know how much I hate that name. You know how much I loathe and despise that name, you damn bitch."

"Our mother named her after herself," Esther said.

"She should have named you Vera. You're the damn Vera. I'm not that damn person. I'm just me. You're the Vera. You're more her than I am."

"She gets this way, Gary. It's a real laugh and a half, isn't it?"

"You're the only damn Vera in the vicinity that I know of. It's the honest-to-goddest truth, Gary. She's the damn Vera, not me."

"Quiet," I said.

"We can all go live somewhere in Mexico," Myna said. "We can live in a house in the mountains with a garden that's always full of flowers, the wildest colors in Mexico. We can buy a Rolls-Royce and go. Gary, you drive."

"We can buy four Rolls-Royces," Esther said.

"You don't need all that money to go to Mexico and live in a garden," Vera said.

"But we're getting four Rolls-Royces."

"I think we should get just one," Myna said. "That way we stay together."

"That's right," Vera said.

"That way we insure staying together. And we can all study the works of Tudev Nemkhu who's this Mongolian science-fiction writer who's got a real big underground following. He's in exile in Libya because his government frowns on sci-fi."

"All of us in the mountains smoking our little pipes," Vera said.

We sat around for a while longer. Myna read to us, bouncing on her haunches, pausing after certain passages to bite her nails. We heard the wind then. It came up suddenly, fanning sand into the air. We tried to cover ourselves. Esther wore a large button with the word CAR-ROTS printed on it.

18

THE FOOTBALL TEAM filled two buses and rode a hundred and twenty miles to a point just outside the campus of the West Centrex Biotechnical Institute. There the buses split up, offense to one motel, defense to another. We had steak for dinner and went to our rooms. All evening we kept visiting each other, trying to talk away the nervousness. Finally Sam Trammel and Oscar Veech came around and told us to get to bed. There were three men to a room. The regulars got beds; the substitutes were assigned to cots. Bloomberg and I had a reserve guard, Len Skink, sharing our room. For some reason Len was known as Dog-Boy. In the darkness I listened to the cars going by. I knew I'd have trouble sleeping. A long time passed, anywhere from an hour to three hours or more.

"Is anybody awake?" Len said.

"I am."

"Who's that?" he said.

"Gary."

"You scared me. I didn't think anybody would be awake. I'm having trouble sleeping. Where's Bloomers?"

"He's in bed."

"He doesn't make a sound," Len said. "I can't hear a single sound coming from his bed. A big guy like that."

"That means he's asleep."

"It's real dark in here, isn't it? It's as dark with your eyes open as when they're closed. Put your hand in front of your face. I bet you can't see a thing. My hand is about three inches from my face and I can't see it at all. How far is your hand, Gary?"

"I don't know. I can't see it."

"We better get some sleep. This stuff isn't for me. I remember the night I graduated high school. We stayed up all night. That was some night."

"What did you do?"

"We stayed up," he said.

In the morning we went out to the stadium, suited up without pads or headgear and had an extra mild workout, just getting loose, tossing the ball around, awakening our bodies to the feel of pigskin and turf. The place seemed fairly new. It was shaped like a horseshoe and probably seated about 22,000. Our workout progressed in virtual silence. It was a cool morning with no breeze to speak of. We went back in and listened to the coaches for a while. Then we rode back to the motels. At four o'clock we had our pregame meal—beef consommé, steak and eggs. At five-thirty we went back out to the stadium and slowly, very slowly, got suited up in fresh uniforms. Nobody said much until we went through the runway and took the field for our warmup. In the runway a few people made their private sounds, fierce alien noises having nothing to do with speech or communication of any kind. It was a kind of frantic breathing with elements of chant, each man's sound unique and yet mated to the other sounds, a mass rhythmic breathing that became more widespread as we emerged from the runway and trotted onto the field. We did light calisthenics and ran through some basic plays. Then the receivers and backs ran simple pass patterns as the quarterbacks took turns throwing. Off to the side the linemen exploded from their stances, each one making his private noise, the chant or urgent breathing of men in preparation for ritual danger. We returned to the locker room in silence and listened to our respective coaches issue final instructions. Then I put on my helmet and went looking for Buddy Shock. He and the other line-backers were still being lectured by Vern Feck. I waited until the coach was finished and then I grabbed Buddy by the shoulder, spun him around and hit him with a forearm across the chest, hard. He answered with three open-hand blows against the side of my helmet.

"Right," I said. "Right, right, right."

"Awright. Aw-*right,* Gary boy."

"Right, right, right."

"Awright, aw-*right.*"

"Get it up, get it in."

"Work, work, work."

"Awright."

"Awright. Aw-riiiight."

I walked slowly around the room, swinging my arms over my head. Some of the players were sitting or lying on the floor. I saw Jerry Fallon and approached him. He was standing against a wall, fists clenched at his sides, his helmet on the floor between his feet.

"Awright, Jerry boy."

"Awright, Gary."

"We move them out."

"Huh huh huh."

"How to go, big Jerry."

"Huh huh huh."

"Awright, awright, awright."

"We hit, we hit."

"Jerry boy, big Jerry."

Somebody called for quiet. I turned and saw Emmett Creed standing in front of a blackboard at the head of the room. His arms were crossed over his chest and he held his baseball cap in his right hand. It took only a few seconds before the room was absolutely still. The cap dangled from his fingers.

"I want the maximal effort," he said.

Then we were going down the runway, the sounds louder now, many new noises, some grunts and barks, everyone with his private noise, hard fast rhythmic sounds. We came out of the mouth of the tunnel and I saw the faces looking down from both sides, the true, real

and honest faces, Americans on a Saturday night, even
the more well-to-do among them bearing the look of
sharecroppers, a vestigial line of poverty wearing thin but
still present on every face, the teen-agers looking like
prewar kids, 1940, poorly cut short hair and a belligerent
cleanliness. After the introductions I butted pads with
Bobby Hopper and then bounced up and down on the
sideline as we won the coin toss. The captains returned
and we all gathered together around Creed, all of us
making noises, a few prayers said, some obscenities exchanged, men jumping, men slapping each other's helmets. Creed said something into all the noise and then the
kick-return team moved onto the field. I glanced across at
Centrex. They looked big and happy. They were wearing
red jerseys with silver pants and silver helmets. We wore
white jerseys with green pants and green and white helmets. My stomach was tight; it seemed to be up near my
chest somewhere. I was having trouble breathing and an
awful sound was filling my helmet, a sound that seemed to
be coming from inside my head. I could see people getting
up all over the stadium and the cheerleaders jumping and
a couple of stadium cops standing near an exit. I could
see the band playing, the movements of the band mem-
bers as they played, but I couldn't hear the music. I
looked down to my right. Bobby Iselin and Taft Robinson
were the deep men. Speed and superspeed. About sixty-
eight yards upfield the kicker raised his right arm, gave a
little hop, and began to move toward the ball.

Part Two

19

THE SPECIAL TEAMS collided, swarm and thud of inter-
changeable bodies, small wars commencing here and
there, exaltation and firstblood, a helmet bouncing bright-
ly on the splendid grass, the breathless impact of two
destructive masses, quite pretty to watch.

(The spectator, at this point, is certain to wonder
whether he must now endure a football game in print—
the author's way of adding his own neat quarter-notch to
the scarred bluesteel of combat writing. The game, after
all, is known for its assault-technology motif, and numer-
ous commentators have been willing to risk death by
analogy in their public discussions of the resemblance
between football and war. But this sort of thing is of little
interest to the exemplary spectator. As Alan Zapalac says
later on: "I reject the notion of football as warfare. Warfare is warfare. We don't need substitutes because we've
got the real thing." The exemplary spectator is the person
who understands that sport is a benign illusion, the
illusion that order is possible. It's a form of society that is
rat-free and without harm to the unborn; that is organized
so that everyone follows precisely the same rules; that is
electronically controlled, thus reducing human error and
benefiting industry; that roots out the inefficient and pe-
nalizes the guilty; that tends always to move toward perfection. The exemplary spectator has his occasional lusts,
but not for warfare, hardly at all for that. No, it's details
he needs—impressions, colors, statistics, patterns, mys-

teries, numbers, idioms, symbols. Football, more than othe
sports, fulfills this need. It is the one sport guided b
language, by the word signal, the snap number, the colo
code, the play name. The spectator's pleasure, when no
derived from the action itself, evolves from a notion of th
game's unique organic nature. Here is not just order bu
civilization. And part of the spectator's need is to sort th
many levels of material: to allot, to compress, to cata
logue. This need leaps from season to season, devourin
much of what is passionate and serene in the spectator
He tries not to panic at the final game's final gun. H
knows he must retain something, squirrel some food fo
summer's winter. He feels the tender need to survive th
termination of the replay. So maybe what follows is
form of sustenance, a game on paper to be scanned whe
there are stale days between events; to be propped up and
looked at—the book as television set—for whatever is i
here of terminology, pattern, numbering. But maybe not
It's possible there are deeper reasons to attempt a play
by-play. The best course is for the spectator to continue
forward, reading himself into the very middle of tha
benign illusion. The author, always somewhat corrupt i
his inventions and vanities, has tried to reduce the contes
to basic units of language and action. Every beginning, i
is assumed, must have a neon twinkle of danger about it
and so grandmothers, sissies, lepidopterists and others are
warned that the nomenclature that follows is often indeci
pherable. This is not the pity it may seem. Much of the
appeal of sport derives from its dependence on elegan
gibberish. And of course it remains the author's perma
nent duty to unbox the lexicon for all eyes to see—
cryptic ticking mechanism in search of a revolution.)

Blue turk right, double-slot, zero snag delay.

I was the lone setback. Nobody took out their middl
linebacker. I got hit at the line of scrimmage, the 31,
high hard shot that settled my stomach and got rid of th
noise in my head. Hobbs threw to Jessup on a half-moo

pattern good for twelve. Taft went outside for six yards, then three, then five. I went straight ahead for five. Taft took a trigger pitch, cut inside a good block and went to their 22. We left the huddle with a sharp handclap and trotted up to the line, eager to move off the ball, sensing a faint anxiety on the other side of the line.

Quick picket left, hook right.
Twin option off modified crossbow.
Re-T, chuck-and-go.

"How to hit," George Dole shouted out to us. "Way to pop, way to go, way to move. How to sting them, big Jerry. Bloomers, Bloomers, Bloomers. How to play this game."

Taft, stutter-stepping, juked a man into the ground and was forced out at the 5. I went off-tackle to the 1. Our line was firing out beautifully. It was crisp basic football. We were playing better than ever, in controlled bursts, probably because we were facing real talent. Taft went into the end zone standing up. Two of the receivers ran after him to slap his helmet and escort him off. Bing Jackmin kicked the extra point. I got down on one knee on the sideline, the chin strap of my helmet undone, material for a prizewinning sports photo. Commotion everywhere. Oscar Veech was shouting into my left ear.

"Gary, on the thirty-two I want you to catapult out of there. I want you to really come. I want to see you zoom into the secondary. But be sure you protect that ball."

"Right."

"Get fetal, get fetal."

"Fetal," I shouted back.

Centrex returned the kickoff to their 27. Our defense rolled into a gut 4–3 with variable off-picks. Their quarterback, Telcon, moved them on the ground past midfield, then went to the air on two of the next three plays. They tried a long field goal, wide to the right, and we took over. Hobbs hit Spurgeon Cole for good yardage but we were caught holding. Taft picked up eight. Ron Steeples was knocked cold and we were forced to call a time-out to get him off. Chuck Deering came running in to replace him, tripping and falling as he reached the huddle. I went inside tackle for three yards. Hobbs threw to Taft on a gate-delay out of the backfield. It picked up only seven and the punting team came on. I sat on the bench, noticing Raymond Toon down at the far end; he seemed to be talking into his fist. Byrd Whiteside punted to their 44, a fair catch. Telcon moved them on the ground, inside mostly, all the way to our 19. Dennis Smee kicked somebody. That moved the ball inside the 10. Three running plays. The extra point tied it.

When we huddled at the 24, Hobbs said: "Stem left, L and R hitch and cross, F weak switch and sideline. On hut."

"What?" Chuck Deering said.

"On hut."

"No, the other thing. F something."

"F weak switch and sideline," Hobbs said.

"What kind of pattern is that?"

"Are you kidding?"

"What a bunch of fetus-eaters," Kimbrough said.

"When did they put that pattern in, Hobbsie?"

"Tuesday or Wednesday. Where the hell were you?"

"It must have been Wednesday. I was at the dentist."

"Nobody told you?"

"I don't think so, Hobbsie."

"Look, you run out ten yards, put some moves on your man and end up near the damn sideline."

"I'm co-captain to a bunch of fetus-eaters."

"On hut. Break."

Third and eleven. They sent their linebackers. Hobbs left the pocket and I had Mallon, their psychotic middle linebacker, by the jersey. He tripped and I released, moving into a passing plane for Hobbs. He saw me but threw low. I didn't bother diving for it. Creed seemed to be looking right past us as we moved off the field. I sat next to Chester Randall, a reserve lineman. He had broken his right wrist the week before and it was still in a cast.

"Make no mistake, I can play with this thing. Hauptfuhrer gave me the go. If they need me, I can play, arm or no arm. The only thing that worries me is the dryness. I wish I could spit. I'm too dry to spit. I've been trying to work up some saliva for the past hour. I'd feel a whole lot better if I could only spit."

"Why don't you drink some water?"

"I've been trying to avoid that. It's what killed my sister's baby. There's something in it."

Centrex, starting from midfield, picked up six, eight, five, four, nine. Lenny Wells came off in pain—his left arm. George Owen screamed at him. The quarter ended. I thought of ice melting above the banks of streams in high country. Billy Mast replaced Wells. Telcon kept the ball on a bootleg and went to the 1 (flag in the air) before Buddy Shock caught him with a shoulder. Their penalty, clipping, and that put the ball outside the 20 from point of infraction. Telcon tried to hit his flanker on a post pattern. Bobby Iselin picked it off and returned to the 19. I couldn't find my helmet for a moment.

Garland Hobbs: "Let's ching those nancies."

Monsoon sweep, string-in left, ready right.
Cradle-out, drill-9 shiver, ends chuff.
Broadside option, flow-and-go.

I got bounced out of bounds and stepped on. Veech shouted down at me. Hard-earned first down for the unspectacular Harkness. Taft ran out of room and cut back into traffic. Their territory, second and eight. Hobbs looked toward Creed for guidance. The man's arms remained folded, his right foot tamping the grass.

Quickside brake and swing.

I put a light block on their end, then turned to the right to watch the play develop. Taft caught the ball about six yards behind the line and followed the center and both guards. They looked impressive, trucking along out there in front, Onan Moley flanked by Rector and Fallon, but nobody remembered to throw a block. The left cornerback sliced in to make an ankle-high tackle just as Taft was getting set to turn it on. A Centrex lineman was hurt, knee or ankle, and they had to call time to get him off. We assembled near our own 45. John Jessup took off his helmet. There was blood all over his lips and teeth.

"Nobody got taken out on that brake and swing," Hobbs said.

"You just call the blankety-blank signals," Kimbrough said. "We'll do the blocking."

"When do you plan to start?"

"Suck a husky," Fallon said.

"That ass-belly sixty-two got his fist in," Jessup said. "That magnolia candy-ass cunt."

"You'd better go off."

"I guarantee you I'll mash his little mimmy. I'm serious, man. I'll waste that diddly dick before this thing's over."

"Go off," I said. "Your mouth is all over your face. You're making everybody sick."

"I'll get that shitpiss sixty-two and smash his worthless face."

"Down and yardage," Cecil Rector said.

"Third and long," Deering said.

"Are there any predictions on the outcome?" Bloomberg said.

"Be serious," Onan told him.

Their linebackers seemed about to swarm-drop. Hobbs shouted numbers and colors over the defensive signals. I noticed that the knuckles on my left hand were all torn up. Hobbs kept changing plays, reacting to the defense. The whistle blew, delay of game, and we rehuddled and came back out. Hobbs threw to Spurgeon Cole up the middle. He got hit and dropped it. Centrex claimed fumble but the official paid no attention. Byrd Whiteside punted miserably. When he came off, Tweego told him he looked like something that had just come inching out of a buffalo's ass. I sat next to Bing Jackmin on the bench.

"I wonder what we're missing on TV," he said.

Centrex stayed on the ground, going mainly over our left side, Lloyd Philpot and Champ Conway. On first down Telcon faked a hand-off, rolled right and hit one of his backs, number 25, all alone in the end zone. The conversion was good and our kick-return team left the bench. Bobby Iselin returned to the 17 where he was hit and fumbled. Lee Roy Tyler recovered for us. I jogged onto the field.

Each play must have a name. The naming of plays is important. All teams run the same plays. But each team uses an entirely different system of naming. Coaches stay up well into the night in order to name plays. They heat and reheat coffee on an old burner. No play begins until its name is called.

Middle-sift-W, alph-set, lemmy-2.

Taft went burning up the middle for fifteen. He got six on the next play. I was up ahead, blocking, and we went down along with three or four other people. I was on my back, somebody across my legs, when I realized their tackle, 77, was talking to me, or to Taft, or perhaps to all of us spread over the turf. He was an immense and very geometric piece of work, their biggest man, about six-seven and 270, an oblong monument to the virtues of intimidation. His full hazy eyes squinted slowly deep inside the helmet as he whispered over the grass.

"Nigger kike faggot. Kike fag. Kike. Nigger fag. Nigger kike faggot."

Hobbs faked a trigger pitch to Taft, then handed to me, a variation off the KC draw. Mike Mallon and I met head-on. I went down a bit faster than he did. Hobbs called for a measurement although we were obviously short, almost a yard. I was breathing heavily as we rehuddled. I thought one or two ribs might be broken. Taft went straight ahead, bounced off Onan Moley and tried to take it outside. A linebacker grabbed his jersey, somebody else held him upright and then 77 stormed into him. I knew we had lost yardage and I took off my helmet and started off. I heard a scuffle behind me. I put my helmet back on. It was Jessup and number 62 ready to go at each other. Bloomberg moved between them and they started to circle him, cursing each other. Then somebody pushed 62 away and Anatole took Jessup by the arm and led him off. About ten yards away Taft was just getting to his feet. Tweego had Cecil Rector by the pads as I crossed the sideline.

"I want you to fire out, boy. You're not blowing them out. You're not popping. I want you to punish that man. I want you to straighten him up and move him out. You're not doing any of those things."

I watched Creed take one very long step to the side in order to bring Cecil within hearing range. He spoke to Cecil while looking straight out toward the field, as if even the chaos of offensive and defensive units moving in and out was infinitely more noteworthy than this well-balanced arrangement of armor and flesh.

"You're too nice, son."

"Yes sir."

"You're not firing out," Tweego yelled. "That man is

raping you. He is moving you at will. Sting him, goddamn it. Sting him. Sting him."

"You're just too damn nice," Creed said.

Moving on the ground, Centrex picked up three, eight, nine, then lost four on a good tackle by Dennis Smee who went spinning off a block and hit the ballcarrier very hard around the midsection as he hesitated while bellying out on a sweep. Third and five. Telcon rolled out, got set to throw, saw his man covered, sidestepped Dickie Kidd and reversed his field. Buddy Shock just missed him way behind the line. Howard Lowry grabbed an ankle and then John Billy Small was all over Telcon. He seemed to be climbing him. They both went down on top of Lowry. Punt formation. Bobby Hopper called for a fair catch. My ribs seemed all right and and I went out. Three firecrackers went off in the stands. The crowd responded with prolonged applause.

Taft took a quick toss at the point and followed me inside their left end. Then I was down and somebody was running right over me. I heard a lot of noise, pads hitting, men grunting and panting. Then it all came down on top of me. I smelled the turf and waited for the bodies to unpile. My rib cage was beginning to ache, a sense of stickiness, of glue. I felt quite happy. Somebody's hand was at the back of my neck and he put all his weight on it as he lifted himself up.

Counter-freeze, blue-2 wide, swing inside delay.

I flared to the left, taking Mallon with me. Taft waited for a two-count and swung over the middle. Under pressure Hobbs threw high. Third and four. I couldn't contain my man. I tried to hold him. Then he and two others were all over Hobbs. I walked off without looking back. Whiteside punted sixty yards in the air. Jeff Elliott moved along the bench toward me.

"We're not moving the ball."

"I know," I said.

"That first drive was tremendous, Gary. But since then."

"We'll probably get killed. I anticipate a final score of eighty-three to seven."

"Not this team. This is a real team. We've got the character to come back. We're only down seven. This is a team that goes out and plays."

"I was just talking, Jeff. Psyching myself."

"That's some way to psych yourself. How you feeling? Let me see that hand."

"I'm feeling happy," I said. "Look at the arc lights, the crowd. Listen to those noises out there. Pop, pop, pop. Ving, ving. Existence without anxiety. Happiness. Knowing your body. Understanding the real needs of man. The real needs, Jeffrey."

"I just meant your hand. It's all gouged up."

"The universe was born in violence. Stars die violently. Elements are created out of cosmic violence."

"Gary, this is football."

"I'm just fooling around, Jeff. I'm not serious."

"This team can come back. That's what all the pain and the struggle was for back there last summer. To give us the character to come back."

"Quite right."

"I believe in Coach," Jeff said. "He'll tell us what to do. Wait till half time. Coach will make adjustments."

Telcon hit his tight end near the sideline for twelve. Champ Conway came off holding his left shoulder and John Butler replaced him. Telcon completed two, missed one, hit one. He shook off Link Brownlee and threw to one of his backs who was just lounging around in the flat. The man took it all the way to our 17 before Bobby Luke caught him from behind. They picked up two on the ground, not very stylishly, Kidd and Lowry driving the ballcarrier back about ten yards while the official chased them blowing his whistle. Telcon overthrew a man in the end zone. Then he hit number 29 coming out of the backfield. Butler and Billy Mast put him down at the 9. They called time and Telcon looked toward his bench. Their head coach, Jade Kiley, turned to one of his assistants and said something. I looked at the clock. The field-goal team came on. Hauptfuhrer started shouting at the defense, howling at them. His face was contorted, squeezed into tense pieces. Sound of lamentation. It drifted across the clear night to all bright creatures curled beneath the moon.

"Look out for the fake. Look out for the faaaaake. Aaaaaake. Aaaaaake. Aaaaaake."

They made the field goal. Bobby Iselin returned the kickoff to the 24. We all hurried out.

"Bed," Jerry Fallon said. "Pillow, sheet, blanket, mattress, spring, frame, headboard."

Hobbs hit Chuck Deering on a pony-out for nine. He worked the other sideline and Spurgeon Cole was forced out after picking up thirteen. The bench was shouting encouragement. Hobbs came back with an opp-flux draw to Taft that picked up only two. He called time and went over to talk to Creed. I got my cleats scraped clean and watched Hobbs come trotting back; he seemed to have the answer to everything. I swung behind Deering, who was running a Q-route to clear out the area, and then I fanned toward the sideline and turned. The ball looked beautiful. It seemed overly large and bright. I could see it with perfect clarity. I backed up half a step, leaning with the ball. Then I had it and turned upfield. Somebody grabbed my ankle but I kicked away and picked up speed again, being sure to stay near the sideline. Two of them moved in now. They had the angle on me and I stepped out of bounds. I got hit and dropped and hit again. I came up swinging. Somebody pulled my jersey and I was kicked two or three times in the leg. I realized this was their side of the field. Fallon and Jessup pulled me away. The roughing cost them fifteen and that moved the ball inside their 20. Hobbs hit Cole on a spoon-out to the 10 and we called time. He went off to confer with Creed again. Ron Steeples, who'd been knocked unconscious in the first quarter, came running in now to replace Chuck Deering. He was happy to be back. The scent of grass and dirt filled my nostrils. Hobbs returned and we huddled. His primary receiver was Jessup on a shadow-count delay over the middle. I went into motion and the ball was snapped. I watched Jessup fake a block and come off the line. Hobbs looked to his left, pump-faked, turned toward Jessup and fired. The ball went off Jessup's hand and right to their free safety, 46, who was standing on the goal line. We all stood around watching, either startled or pensive, trying to retrace events. Then 46 decided to take off, evading Kimbrough and Rector, cutting inside me. I went after him at top speed. At the 30-yard line I became aware of something behind me, slightly off to the side. White and green and coming on. Then it was past me, 22, Taft Robinson, running deftly and silently, a remarkable clockwork intactness, smoothly touring, no waste or independent movement. I didn't believe a man could run that fast or well. I slowed down and took off my helmet. Taft caught 46 just the other side of midfield, hitting him below the shoulders and then rolling off and getting to his feet in one motion. I stood there watching. The gun sounded and we all headed for the tunnel.

I sat on the floor sucking the sweet flesh out of half an orange. Onan Moley slid down the wall and settled next to me. Somebody's blood was all over the tape on his forearm.

"We're hitting pretty good." he said. "They're just hitting better."

"They don't do anything unexpected. But they're the kind of team that gets stronger and stronger. They'll demolish us in the second half. They'll just keep coming

They'll keep getting stronger. I figure the final score to be about sixty-six to seven."

"That bad?" Onan said.

"Worse maybe."

"We'll probably have to use cable blocking more often than not in the second half."

"Imagine what it's like," I said, "to go against a major power. These people come on and on. So imagine what it must be like to go against a really major power."

"Yeah, think what it must be like to take the field against Tennessee or Ohio State or Texas."

"Against Notre Dame or Penn State."

"The Fighting Irish," Onan said. "The Nittany Lions."

"Imagine what it must be like to play before a hundred thousand people in the L.A. Coliseum."

"And nationwide TV."

"UCLA versus LSU."

"One of the all-time intersectional dream games."

"We'll never make it," I said. "We'll never even get out of here alive. They'll just keep coming and coming."

"That fifty-five is the meanest thing I ever hope to play against."

"Mallon," I said.

"That thing is clubbing me to death. He rears back and clubs me with a forearm every play. I start wincing as soon as I snap the damn ball because I know old fifty-five is already bringing that forearm around to club my head. Gary, I only go about one ninety-eight. That thing is easy two thirty-five."

"And still growing."

"I guarantee you I'm not about to get him any madder than he was the day he was born. I can take sixty minutes of clubbing as long as I know I'll never see that guy again. He is one mean person, place or thing."

The coaches started yelling for their people. Onan went over to Tweego's group and I went to the blackboard where Oscar Veech and Emmett Creed were waiting.

Creed spoke slowly and evenly, looking from Hobbs to Taft to me, ignoring the other quarterbacks and running backs gathered behind us. Bobby Hopper asked a question about the blocking assignments just put in for the drag slant right. Creed looked at Oscar Veech. It was rather strange. He didn't want to talk to anyone who couldn't help him win.

"Right guard blocks down," Veech said. "Harkness takes out the end."

It wasn't time to go back out yet. I went and sat against another wall. Mitchell Gorse, a reserve safetyman, walked by. In his spotless uniform he looked a bit ludicrous.

"We'll come back, Gary," he said.

"Bullshit."

Across the room Bloomberg was sitting on a park bench that had somehow found its way into the dressing area. From somewhere I could hear Sam Trammel's voice.

"Crackback. Crackback. Crackback."

My helmet, wobbling slightly, rocking, was on the floor between my feet. I looked into it. I felt sleepy and closed my eyes. I went away for a while, just one level down. Everything was far away. I thought (or dreamed) of a sunny green garden with a table and two chairs. There was a woman somewhere, either there or almost there, and she was wearing clothes of another era. There was music. She was standing behind a chair now, listening to a Bach cantata. It was Bach all right. When I lost the woman, the music went away. But it was still nice. The garden was still there and I felt I could add to it or take away from it if I really tried. Just to see if I could do it, I took away a chair. Then I tried to bring back the woman without the music. Somebody tapped my head and I opened my eyes. I couldn't believe where I was. Suddenly my body ached all over. They were getting up and getting ready to move out. I was looking into Roy Yellin's chewed-up face.

"They're putting me in for Rector," he said.

"What's wrong with Cecil?"

"Nothing wrong with Cecil. He's just not hitting. He's getting beat. His man is overpowering him. Number seventy-seven's his man. He looks real big, Gary. Big, strong and mobile. Those are Tweego's exact words. What do you think?"

"His tusks would bring a fortune in Zanzibar."

"He's jamming up the damn middle. Coach just talked to me about it. He said to fire out and really hit. Really chop him up. What do you think, Gary? Supposin' I can't move him? They're counting on me to move that fucking mother animal."

"He'll kill you," I said.

"You think so?"

"He killed Cecil, didn't he? He'll kill you too. He'll drive you right back to the bench. He'll humiliate you, Roy. Coach'll have to send Skink in. He'll be reduced to that. Len Skink. Dog-Boy. He'll have to do it. Because seventy-seven is going to eat your face. You'd better fake an injury the first time we have the ball. It's your only hope. I promise I won't let on. If you try to play against that big horrible thing, he'll send you home in pieces. He did it to Cecil and he'll do it to you. Look, Roy, I'm just kidding. It helps me relax."

"Are you serious?"

"I'm kidding."

"That's what I mean."

"You'll do the job, Roy. I just said those things to undermine my sense of harmony. It's very complex. It has to do with the ambiguity of this whole business."

I got up and punched a locker. It was almost time. I didn't expect Creed to have any final words and I realized I was right when I saw George Owen get up on a chair. His gaze moved slowly across the room, then back again. He held his clenched fists against the sides of his head. Slowly, his knees began to bend.

"Cree-unch," he said softly. "Cree-unch. Creech. Crunch."

We started to make noises.

"You know what to do," he said, and his voice grew louder. "You know what this means. You know where we are. You know who to get."

We were all making the private sounds. We were getting ready. We were getting high. The noise increased in volume.

"Footbawl," George Owen shouted. "This is footbawl. You thow it, you ketch it, you kick it. Footbawl. Footbawl. Footbawl."

We were running through the tunnel out onto the field. Billy Mast and I met at the sideline. He raised his hands above his head and then brought them down on my pads—one, two, three times. I jumped up and down and threw a shoulder into Billy. The band marched off now. We were both jumping up and down, doing private and almost theological calisthenics, bringing God into the frenzied body, casting out fear.

"How to go, little Billy."

"Hiyoto, hiyoto."

"They're out to get us. They'll bleach our skulls with hydrosulfite."

"They'll rip off our clothes and piss on our bare feet."

"Yawaba, yawaba, yawaba."

"How to go, Gary boy. How to jump, how to jump."

"They'll twist our fingers back."

"They'll kill us and eat us."

Centrex came out. We gathered around Creed again and then broke with a shout. The kickoff team went on. Bing Jackmin kicked to the 7 or 8 and they returned to the 31 where Andy Chudko hit the ballcarrier at full force and then skidded on his knees over the fallen player's body. I watched Creed take his stance at the midfield stripe. Bing Jackmin came off the field and sat next to me.

"One two three a-nation. I received my confirmation. On the day of declaration. One two three a-nation."

"They're coming out in a double-wing," I said.

"It's all double, Gary. Double consciousness. Old form superimposed on new. It's a breaking-down of reality. Primitive mirror awareness. Divine electricity. The football feels. The football knows. This is not just one thing we're watching. This is many things."

"You know what Coach says. It's only a game but it's the only game."

"Gary, there's a lot more out there than games and players."

Telcon faked a hand-off, dropped slowly back (ball on his hip), then lofted a pass to his flanker who had five steps on Bobby Luke. The ball went through his hands, a sure six, and he stood on our 45-yard line just a bit stunned, his hands parted, a tall kid with bony wrists, looking upfield to the spot in time and space he would have been occupying that very second if only he had caught the football. They sagged a little after that and had to punt. Bobby Hopper called for a fair catch and fumbled. About six players fought for possession, burrowing, crawling, tearing at the ground. A Centrex player leaped out of the mass, his fist in the air, and their offense came back on. Lee Roy Tyler limped to the sideline. Vern Feck stomped his clipboard, then turned his back to the field and looked beyond our bench, way out over the top of the stadium. From our 32 they picked up two, one and five on the ground. Telcon looked across at his head coach. We rose from the bench and crowded near the sideline. Centrex broke and set.

Hauptfuhrer chanted to his linemen: "Contain. Contain. Contain those people. Infringe. Infringe on them. Rape that man, Link. Rape him. Ray-yape that man."

Dennis Smee, at middle linebacker, shouted down at

the front four: "Tango-two. Reset red. Hoke that bickie. Mutt, mutt, mutt."

John Butler fought off a block and held the ballcarrier upright at the 23. We made noises at the defense as they came off. Hobbs opened with a burn-7 hitch to Ron Steeples off the fake picket. Second and one. Hobbs used play-action and threw to Spurgeon Cole, seam-X-in, leading him too much. Their tight safety came over to pick it off and ran right into Spurgeon. Their ball. Both players down. The safety needed a stretcher. Spurgeon came off on his own and then collapsed. I moved away from him, putting on my helmet as I watched Centrex move toward the line. A moment later I glanced over. The trainer was kneeling over Spurgeon and soon he was up and shaking his head. I took my helmet off. I patted him on the leg as he went by. He grinned down at me, a great raw grassy bruise on his left cheekbone.

"Crash," he said.

"You're all right."

"Ca-rash."

Telcon threw twice for first downs. Two holding penalties moved them back. They tried two draws. Then Buddy Shock turned a reverse inside. They punted dead on our 23. I went out, feeling the glue spreading over my ribs. Hobbs called a power 26 off the crossbow with Taft Robinson carrying. I went in low at their left end. He drove me to my knees and I grabbed an ankle and pulled. On his way down he put a knee into my head.

Out-23, near-in belly toss.

Taft barely made it to the line of scrimmage. On a spring-action trap I went straight ahead, careened off 77 and got leveled by Mike Mallon. He came down on top of me, breathing into my face, chugging like a train. I closed my eyes. The noise of the crowd seemed miles away.

Through my jersey the turf felt chilly and hard. I heard somebody sigh. A deep and true joy penetrated my being. I opened my eyes. All around me there were people getting off the ground. Directly above were the stars, elucidations in time, old clocks sounding their chimes down the bending universe. I regretted knowing nothing about astronomy; it would have been pleasant to calculate the heavens. Bloomberg was leaning over to help me to my feet. We joined the huddle. Garland Hobbs on one knee spoke into the crotches of those who faced him.

"Brown feather right, thirty-one spring-T. On two. Break."

I couldn't believe it. The same play. The same play, I thought. He's called the same play. A fairly common maneuver, it somehow seemed rhapsodic now. How beautiful, I thought. What beauty. What a beautiful thing to do. Hobbs received the snapback, Roy Yellin pulled, and there I was with the football, the pigskin, and it was planted once more in my belly and I was running to daylight, to starlight, and getting hit again by Mallon, by number 55, by their middle linebacker, by five-five, snorting as he hit me, an idiotically lyrical moment. Down I went, the same play, the grass and stars. It's all taking so long, I thought. The galaxy knows itself. The quasars repeat their telling of time. Nine tenths of the universe is missing. I was covered with large people. In a short while they raised themselves and I drifted back to the huddle. The chains came out. First down. Hobbs overthrew Jessup, then Steeples. Taft went wide for two. Centrex returned the punt to their 33.

Ted Joost squatted next to me on the sideline.

"This whole game could be played via satellite. They could shoot signals right down here. We'd be equipped with electronic listening devices. Transistor things sealed into our headgear. We'd receive data from the satellites and run our plays accordingly. The quarterback gets one set of data. The linemen get blocking patterns. The receivers get pass routes. Ek cetera. Same for the defense. Ek cetera."

"Who sends the data?" I said.

"The satellites."

"Who feeds the satellites?"

"A computer provides the necessary input. There'd be a computerized data bank of offensive plays, of defensive formations, of frequencies. What works best against a six-one on second down and four inside your own thirty? The computer tells the satellite. The satellite broadcasts to the helmet. There'd be an offensive satellite and a defensive satellite."

Centrex stayed on the ground. Their guards and tackles came off the ball. Dickie Kidd was helped off and George Dole replaced him. They picked up nine, four, eight, three, three, six. They moved quickly in and out of the huddle. They kept grinding it out. They kept hitting, they kept moving. Billy Mast's jersey was torn off his back and he had to come off for a new one. He removed his helmet. Both his eyes were puffed up and there was a patch of dry blood at the corner of his mouth. Telcon skirted John Butler and picked up two key blocks. Bobby Iselin bumped him out at the 16.

Vern Feck to Butler: "Shitbird. Shitbird. Shitbird. Shit."

Our defense called time to get organized. Larry Nix went in for Lloyd Philpot. I watched Lloyd come toward the bench. His jersey wasn't tucked into his pants. Tape was hanging from his left wrist and hand. He squatted down between Ted Joost and me.

"I didn't infringe. The coaches wanted optimum infringement. But I didn't do the job. I didn't infringe."

Two running plays gained little or nothing. Then Telcon got pressure from Howard Lowry and had to throw the ball away. Their field-goal kicker came on. The ball hit the crossbar and bounced back.

Delta-3 series, saddleback-in, shallow hinge reverse. Span-out option, jumbo trap.

I followed a good block by Jerry Fallon, tripping over somebody's leg and gaining only three. Then, on a column sweep, Taft turned the corner and picked up speed just as a lane opened and suddenly he was gone, out into open territory, and I watched from my knees as he dipped and swerved and cut past a cornerback, one motion, accelerating off the cut and heading straight for the last man, the free safety, and then veering off just slightly, almost contemptuously, not bothering to waste a good hip-fake, still operating on that first immaculate thrust, cruising downhill from there. I was on my feet and following him. We were all running after him, running past our bench, everybody standing and yelling, jumping, looking at the back of his jersey, at 22 in white and green, the crowd up and screaming—a massive, sustained and somehow lonely roar. I slowed to a walk and watched Taft glide into the end zone. He executed a dainty little curl to the left and casually dropped the football. Moody Kimbrough stumbled over the goal line and picked him up. Then Fallon and Jessup were there and they were all carrying Taft back across the goal line, holding him at the waist and under the arms, and Roy Yellin was jumping up and down and smacking Taft on the helmet. Spurgeon Cole stood beneath the goal posts, repeating them, arms raised in the shape of a crossbar and uprights, his fists clenched. The crowd was still up, leaning, in full voice, addressing its own noise. Taft came off. Bing Jackmin kicked the extra point. I hit Taft on the helmet and sat next to Tim Flanders.

"We got a game going now," he said. "We got a game going. We got a game going now."

"I think my ribs are busted," I said.

"You're okay. You're okay. You're okay."

Bing kicked out of bounds and had to do it over. They returned to the 38. The quarter ended. I went over to hit Taft on the helmet again. Hauptfuhrer and Vern Feck were explaining something about gap-angle blocking to Dennis Smee. Emmett Creed moved his right foot over the grass, a few inches either way. This was his power, to deny us the words we needed. He was the maker of plays, the name-giver. We were his chalk-scrawls. Something like that.

Centrex stayed inside the tackles, making two first downs. Then Telcon handed to his big back, 35, and I watched him come right toward us, toward the bench, rumbling over the turf, really pounding along. He got ready to lower a shoulder as he sensed Buddy Shock coming straight across from his linebacker's spot. They met before the runner could turn upfield. Buddy left his feet as he made contact, coming in hard, swinging a forearm under the lowered shoulder. They went down a few yards away from us. We heard the hard blunt heavy sound of impact and then the wild boar grunt as they hit the ground and bounced slightly, gasping now, breathing desperately, looking into the earth for knowledge and power. Standing above them we watched solemnly, six or seven of us, as Buddy put his hand on the ballcarrier's head and pushed himself upright. Then 35 got to his feet, slowly, still panting. John Jessup spoke to him, conversationally, in a near whisper.

"You're a nipple-prick, thirty-five. You're an eensie-weensie. You got your dong from a cereal box."

"He's barely got a dong," Jim Deering said.

"Nipple-prick. Nipple-prick."

"Eensie, eensie, eensie."

They stayed on the ground, moving to our 16. Telcon rolled out right, threw left. Their tight end, all alone on the 5, walked in with it. I felt tired suddenly. A wave of sorrow passed over our bench. After the extra point, they kicked away from Taft, a low floater that Ted Joost fell on at the 29. Taft picked up three on a rip-slant. Roy Yellin came up limping.

"Walk it off," Kimbrough told him.

"Oh mother," Yellin said. "Oh Grace Porterfield Yellin. Oh it hurts, it hurts."

"Walk it off, shovel-head."

Zone set, triple tex, off-hit recon dive.

I was pass-blocking for Hobbs. The big thing, 77, shed Yellin and came dog-paddling in. I jammed my helmet into his chest and brought it up fast, striking his chin. He made a noise and kept coming, kept mauling me. He backed me up right into Hobbs and we all went down. I heard the coaches screaming, their voices warming our huddle. Hobbs left the pocket and threw to Taft in a crowd. A linebacker tipped it, gained control and brought it in. Taft got a piece of him and Ron Steeples put him down. As we went off, Oscar Veech screamed into our chests.

"What in the hell is going on here? What are you feebs doing out there? What in the goddamn goat-shit hell is the name of the game you people are playing?"

The ball was spotted at our 33. Dennis Smee moved along the line, slapping helmets and pads. Jessup sat next to me on the bench. Blades of grass were stuck to the dry blood on his face. Centrex shifted into a tight-T. Halfback picked up four. Telcon kept for six. Halfback went straight ahead for nine. Halfback went straight ahead for eight. Fullback went off-tackle for four. Fullback went straight ahead, taking George Dole into the end zone with him. The extra point was good.

"Fee-uck," Jessup said.

"It's all over."

"Fee-uck, man. This game is still on. I get that sixty-two yet. I get his ass and whip it into shape. Damnright. I get that shitpiss sixty-two and beat his black ass into the ground."

"He's white," I said.

"I know he's white. They're all white. Everybody's white. Those black fucks."

Taft took the kickoff six yards deep and brought it out to the 44. Len Skink reported in for Yellin. Randy King replaced Onan Moley. Terry Madden came in at quarterback. He hit Taft on a snowbird flare for no gain. He threw deep to Steeples incomplete. He fumbled the snap and fell on it. Bing Jackmin met me at the sideline.

"Our uniforms are green and white," he said. "The field itself is green and white—grass and chalk markings. We melt into our environment. We are doubled in the primitive mirror."

I walked down to the very end of the bench. Raymond Toon was all alone, talking into his right fist.

"There it goes, end over end, a high spiral. The deep man avoids or evades would be better. Down he goes, woof. First and ten at the twenty-six or thirty-one. Now they come out in a flood left to work against a rotating zone."

"Toony, that's not a flood."

"Hey, Gary. Been practicing."

"So have we."

"There they go. Andy Chudko, in now for Butler, goes in high, number sixty-one, Andy Chudko, fumble, fumble, six feet even, about two twenty-five, doubles at center on offense, Chudko, Chudko, majoring in airport commissary management, plays a guitar to relax, no other hobbies, fumble after the whistle. College football—a pleasant and colorful way to spend an autumn afternoon. There goes five, six, seven, eight, nine, ten, eleven yards, big thirty-five, twelve yards from our vantage point here at the Orange Bowl in sun-drenched Miami, Florida. John Billy Small combined to bring him down. John Billy, as they break the huddle, what a story behind this boy, a message of hope and inspiration for all those similarly afflicted, and now look at him literally slicing through those big ballcarriers. Capacity crowd. Emmett Big Bend Creed. Mike Mallon, they call him Mad Dog. Telcon. Multi-talented. A magician with that ball. All the color and excitement. He's got it with a yard to spare off a good block by fifty-three or seventy-three. Woof. Three Rivers Stadium in Pittsburgh or Cincinnati. Perfect weather for football. Time out on the field. And now back to our studios for this message. They're a powerhouse, Gary. They play power football. I'd like to get in there and see what I could do. It looks like some of the guys got banged up pretty bad."

"Nobody's died yet. But then the game isn't over."

"Telcon looks out over the defense. He's a good one. Hut, hut, offside. He's one of the good ones. Plenty of hitting out on that field. I'm sure glad I'm up here. D.C. Stadium in the heart of the nation's capital. Crisp blue skies. Emmett Big Bend Creed. And there's more on tap next week when the Chicago Bears, the monsters of the midway, take on the always rough and tough Green Bay Packers of coach something something. Gary, what's going to happen up there on the banks of the Fox River in little Green Bay when the big bad Bears come blowing in from the windy city?"

"You'd better take it easy," I said. "Try to get a grip on things. I'm serious, Toony. You'd better slow down. I really think you'd better watch yourself."

I went over and sat with Garland Hobbs. Centrex was running sweeps. They picked up a first down at our 38. People began to go home. Somebody in the stands behind us, way up high, was blowing into some kind of air horn. It sent a prehistoric cry across the night, a message of grief from the hills down to the suffering plain. Objects were thrown out of the stands.

"Fug," Hobbs said. "That's all I can say. That's the only word in my head right now. Fug, fug, fug."

Somebody fumbled and Link Brownlee fell on it. I hit Hobbs on the pads and went out. Terry Madden left the pocket, what there was of it, and headed toward the sideline, looking downfield for someone to throw to. Their left end pushed him out of bounds and a linebacker knocked him over the Centrex bench. I strolled over there. Players were milling about, shoving each other just a bit.

Jessup to number 62: "Suckmouth. Peach pit. Shitfinger."

They got fifteen yards for roughing. We went to the near hashmark and huddled. Madden's nose was bleeding. At the snap I moved into my frozen insect pose, ready to pass-block. Jessup ignored his pass route and went right at the linebacker playing over him, 62, leading with a forearm smash to the head and following with a kick in the leg. I watched 62 actually bare his teeth. Soon everybody was in it, swinging fists and headgear, kicking, spitting, holding on to pads, clutching jerseys, both benches emptying now, more objects sailing out of the stands. I was in the very middle of the rocking mass. It was relatively safe there. We were packed too tightly for any serious punching or kicking to be done. The real danger was at the periphery where charges could be made, individual attacks mounted, and I felt quite relaxed where I was, being rocked back and forth. A lot of crazed eyes peered out of the helmets nearby. In the distance I could see some spectators climbing over the guard rails and running onto the field. Then there was a sudden shift in equilibrium and I caught an elbow in the stomach. I turned, noted color of uniform, and started swinging. I moved in for more, very conscious of the man's number,

45, backfield, my size or smaller. Somebody ran into me from behind and I went down. It was impossible to get up. I crawled over bodies and around churning legs. I reached an open area and got to my knees. There was someone standing above me, a spectator, a man in a white linen suit, his hand over his mouth, apparently concealing something, and he seemed to be trying to speak to me, but under the circumstances it was not possible to tell what he was saying or even in what language he was saying it. A player tripped over me; another player, back-pedaling, ended in my lap. Then I was completely buried. By the time I got out, it was just about over. Jessup and 62 were down on the ground, motionless in each other's arms, neither one willing to relinquish his hold. But nobody was fighting now and the officials moved in. It took them about half a minute to persuade Jessup to let go of the other player. I felt all right. My ribs didn't ache for the moment. Both men were thrown out for fighting. The field was cleared. Randy King sat on the grass, trying to get his right shoe back on.

Twin deck left, ride series, white divide.
Gap-angle down, 17, dummy stitch.
Bone country special, double-D to right.

Papers blew across the field. I put a gentle block on their left end, helping out Kimbrough. Madden threw to nobody in particular. The stands were almost empty now. I ran a desultory curl pattern over the middle, putting moves on everybody I passed, including teammates. Madden threw behind me. I reached back with my left hand and pulled it in, a fairly miraculous catch. There was open field for a second. Then I was hit from the side and went down. One of their cornerbacks helped me up. I returned to the huddle. We went to the line and set. The left side of our line was offside. We went back again. Taft ran a near off-bike delay that picked up four. The gun sounded. I walked off the field with newspapers whipping across my legs. We went quietly through the tunnel and into the locker room. We began taking off our uniforms. In front of me, Garland Hobbs took a long red box from the bottom of his dressing area. The label on it read: ALL-AMERICAN QUARTERBACK, A MENDELSOHN-TOPPING SPORTS MOTIVATION CONCEPT. Carefully he opened the box. He arranged twenty-two figurines on a tiny gridiron and then spun a dial. His team moved smartly downfield. Sam Trammel went along the rows of cubicles, asking for complete silence. I assumed a team prayer was forthcoming. Next to me, Billy Mast recited a few German words to himself in the total stillness. When I asked for a translation he said it was just a simple listing of things— house, bridge, fountain, gate, jug, olive tree, window. He said the German words gave him comfort, though not as much as they used to when he didn't know what they meant.

Hauptfuhrer was standing over us.

"Shut up and pray," he said.

Part Three

20

LENNY WELLS WALKED up the aisle toward the rear of the bus. He was wearing his fuzzy white Hibbs & Hannon cowboy hat, a gift from an Oklahoma uncle. He also wore a cast on his left arm, no less a gift judging from the proud look on his face, the sense of self-esteem that noble wounds tend to arouse. Sunlight came through the rear window and he blinked and winced into it, then grinned at Billy Mast and me, spinning into the seat in front of us and turning with the grin on his face and wincing again into the sun.

"They broke it," he said. "It's a clean fracture. Right below the elbow. I saw the x ray. It's broke clean. They broke it all right. No question about it."

"I hate to tell you how many yards they gained rushing," Billy said. "A lot of them right over my frail body."

"I didn't even see the last three quarters," Lenny said. "I was having this thing looked at. Having this thing of mine x-rayed."

"Where's Creed?" I said. "I haven't seen Creed all morning."

The driver closed the door and eased onto the highway. This time there was no separation of offense and defense; the two buses were mixed. Lenny turned toward the front and put the hat down over his eyes. The sun came in through the side windows now. Physically I felt more or less intact. After the game the trainer had looked at my ribs and they were all right, just bruised. Both my legs were bruised also. With the game over I wondered what had made it seem so important. It was nothing now, remembered only by my body, vaguely, in terms of soreness. There were two games still to play but I didn't look forward to them. I realized I had nothing to look forward to, nothing at all. I hoped this was just a momentary postgame depression.

"How's Conway?" I said.

"Collarbone," Billy Mast said. "I don't know how bad. He must be in the other bus. I haven't seen him. But I know it's the collarbone. Kimbrough told me at breakfast. They got the collarbone."

"How's Lee Roy Tyler?"

"Knee. They got the knee. Wrenched knee. Not too bad. He'll be ready."

"What about Randy King?"

"Knee. Knee. They blind-sided him. They got him good. Last play of the game. The blind side. They got the knee. They caved it in on him."

"What about Yellin? How's Yellin? He was really hopping around."

"They got the ankle. They kicked it and then stepped on it. I saw it this morning. The right ankle. It's badly swollen. It's purplish in color. He'll be limping for a few days."

"Dickie Kidd," I said.

"Shoulder separation. Deep bruise on left calf. Latter injury reported to be of particular interest. Star-shaped. Multicolored."

"How'd he get it?"

"Shrapnel," Billy said.

"What about Jessup? Jessup was running around half-mad. Signs of violence were rife."

"He bit his tongue. Fat lip too. Swelling under both eyes. No further comment at this time."

"Who else got what?"

"Bobby Iselin, pulled hamstring. Terry Madden, broken nose. Ron Steeples, mild concussion. Len Skink, worms. Everybody else, assorted contusions and lacerations."

"What about Fallon? I saw them working on Fallon in the training room."

"Fallon. An oversight on my part. Fallon. They got his middle finger."

"What did they do with it?"

"They broke it."

We rode in silence for a while. Jerry Fallon came back and showed us his finger. One of his teeth had been knocked out and he showed us the blank space. I had slept ten hours the night before but I was getting sleepy. Fallon went away and I settled down in the seat. Up front Andy Chudko started strumming his silver guitar. Dennis Smee, the defensive captain, was moving slowly up the aisle, stopping at every seat and saying something to the occupants. As he got closer he took a stick of gum out of his breast pocket and put it in his mouth. Every few seconds his tongue would appear, wrapped in transparent spearmint, and he'd produce a perfect little bubble and then snap it with his front teeth. He was leaning over Chudko now. A sentence entered my mind. I spoke the words with a monotonous intonation.

"Uh, this is maxcom, robomat."

Billy Mast looked at me.

"Robomat, this is maxcom. Do you read?"

"Uh, roger, maxcom," he said.

"You're looking real good, robomat. Is that affirm?"

"Uh, roger. We're looking real good."

"What is your thermal passive mode control?"

"Vector five and locking."

"Uh, what is your inertial thrust correction on fourth and long?"

"We read circularize and nonadjust."

"That is affirm, robomat. You are looking real super on the inset retro deployment thing. We read three one niner five niner. Twelve seconds to adapter vent circuit cutoff."

"Affirmative, maxcom. Three one niner five niner.

Twelve seconds to vent cut. There is God. We have just seen God. He is all around us."

"Uh, roger, robomat. Suggest braking burn and midcourse tracking profile. Auto-path is trans-tandem. Blue and holding."

Dennis Smee reached us now. He looked very sincere. The chewing gum crackled between his teeth. He whispered to us.

"We didn't give it enough. We didn't let it all hang out. But it's over now and we still have two games to play. Next week we find out what we're made of. We have to be big out there. A lot of the guys are hurting. Practically everybody's hurting. But we have to shake it off and come back. We have to guard against a letdown. You can suffer a letdown by winning big or a letdown by losing big. Either way it's dangerous. Kimbrough's over in the other bus saying the exact same thing. We worked it out at breakfast, word for word. That's our function as co-captains. To work for the good of the team."

"Function," Billy said. "A rule of correspondence between two sets related in value and nature to the extent that there is a unique element in one set assigned to each element in the corresponding set, given the respective value differences."

I stepped out of the bus under a strange silverwhite sky. It was awful to be back. There was nothing, absolutely nothing, to look forward to. I went searching for Myna. She was wearing an Icelandic sheep coat, a visored butterscotch cap, her 1930 celluloid bracelet, and tricolored hockey socks.

"I'm trying to be honest here," I said. "I don't know whether I'm serious about liking you or not. Maybe I just like you because it's an odd thing to do. Sometimes I like to do odd things."

"Gary, don't fool around. You know the way I am."

"Okay, I'm sorry."

"Did they hurt you, baby?"

"They killed me," I said.

21

THE NEXT DAY we learned that the athletic department, meaning Creed, had hired a sports information director. Immediately I fashioned a theory based on the relationship between defeat and the need for publicity, or anti-publicity, the elevation of evasive news to the level of literature. The man's name was Wally Pippich, formerly of Wally Pippich Creative Promotion Associates—Reno, Nevada. Later that week he sent word that he wanted to see me. His office was located in the basement of Staley Hall, near the boiler room, in a small corridor where mops and buckets were kept.

Wally was a stubby man with a crew cut and long sideburns. He shook my hand and told me to have a seat. There were cartons and stacks of photographs everywhere. On the floor near my chair were color photos of a roller derby team, a chimpanzee riding a motorcycle through a flaming hoop, and a girl in a bikini surrounded by a bunch of paraplegics holding bowling balls in their laps. In another picture Wally stood with his arm around a young man who wore a gold lamé jumpsuit and held an accordion. Wally wore a straw hat in the picture. The word WHAMO was lettered across the hatband.

"Gary Harkness. Good name. Promotable. I like it. I even love it."

"Thank you."

"Relax and call me Wally."

"Right," I said.

"Tough loss you're coming off. Emmett gave me the

whole scoop. Scoopation. I've known Emmett for seven, eight, nine, ten, eleven years. When my boy gets to be your age, I'm sending him right to Emmett. I don't care if Emmett's coaching in the Arctic Circle—up he goes. Emmett Creed is one hell of a human being. Nothing short of sensational. Am I exaggerating, Gary?"

"Not one iota."

"Let's get down to basics. I've been spending the last few days finding my way around. I've talked to the coaches. I've talked to Emmett. I've even talked to Mrs. Tom. Here's the approach as I conceive it. Taft Robinson and Gary Harkness. The T and G backfield. Taft and Gary. Touch and Go. Thunder and Gore."

"A little word-play. A thing with letters."

"We get the vital stats. We get action photos. We get background stuff. The T and G backfield. We release to newspapers, to sports pubs, to local radio and TV, to the networks. The whole enchilada. Taft Robinson and Gary Harkness. I like the sound of those names. Some names produce a negative gut reaction in my mind. Cyd Charisse. Mohandas K. Gandhi. Xerxes. But Taft-and-Gary has a cute little ring to it. I know I like it and I may even love it."

"So what you're doing then, if I understand you correctly, is a public relations thing, based on football, using Taft and me as spearheads, for the good of the school, more or less."

"Gary, that's as good a capsule summary as I could give myself. See that big carton over there? That carton arrived this morning. Know what's in there? The files of two hundred high school football players. These boys have definite market value. These are C-minus boys or better who are top football players. Now we'll get maybe thirty-five of these boys and give them each a grant. With Emmett's nationwide charisma we'll get a few out-of-state boys as well. Maybe another Taft Robinson or Gary Harkness. And then this tiny little grasshopper institute has a chance to make it big. Bigation. Gary, I'll tell you the honest truth. What I know about football you can inscribe with a blunt crayon around the rim of a shot glass."

"You're not a fan, Wally?"

"I don't know squat about football. I'm an indoors man. But I know the whys and wherefores of the entertainment dollar. People want spectacle plus personality. I've handled country rock freaks. I've handled midget wrestlers. Once I handled a song stylist named Mary Boots Weldon who had her goddamn throat removed because of cancer and kept right on singing out of the little voice box they put in there, croaking out these tearful ballads and drawing bigger crowds than ever. Mary Boots Weldon. Jesus, what an act. I lost my drift. What was I getting at?"

"Wally, I don't understand why you need me as part of this thing. I'm a pretty fair runner and blocker and receiver. Better than average. But Taft is on another level."

"Gary, let me shake your hand. Handation. You're a modest lad and I like that kind of attitude in a business like mine. But you're talking football and I don't know squat about football. I'm talking human interest. I'm talking dramatic balance. I'm talking bang bang—the one-two punch. Look, you've had your problems at schools in the past. I know all about that. I also know you've settled down to become one of the real reliables. Speaking just from the football angle and from all I could gather from the various sources I've been in touch with around here, it's frankly pretty obvious that you know how to comport yourself in every aspect of the game."

"Well," I said.

"No, I'm serious, Gary. You can do it all."

"Thank you."

"No, I mean it. You can really do it all."

"Thanks, Wally."

"No, I really mean it. You're one of the team leaders."

"Right."

"No, I wouldn't lie to you, Gary. The word on you is the same everywhere I turn. Gary Harkness? Gary Harkness can do it all."

"I think you'd be better off concentrating on Taft."

"I like your attitude, Gary. I like the way you comport yourself. This thing's going to work out real fine. Emmett's behind me one hundred and ten percent. That's the kind of man he is. I'd stand up and speak out for Emmett Creed in any public place in the country. And I'm sure you'd do the same. Gary, you're everything they told me you were. Let me shake your goddamn hand."

22

AFTER OUR EIGHTH game, which we won easily, I finished showering and went to my cubicle to get dressed. Lloyd Philpot Jr., wearing a jockstrap and red socks, was waiting for me.

"I have to talk to you," he said.

"Sure."

"I have some information I want to pass along."

"Okay."

"There might be a queer on the squad."

"A queer," I said.

"I found out about it just before we left here at half time. Roy Yellin told me about it. He told me to keep it quiet until we can decide what to do."

"I guess Yellin heard it from Onan. I think I heard Onan mention it once."

"Yellin heard it from Rush."

"Who's Rush?"

"Mike Rush. One of the marginal players. A fringe guy. He's been out with groin damage."

"Okay," I said. "So who's the queer?"

"I don't know," Lloyd said. "I just know there is one."

"But Yellin didn't tell you who it is."

"Yellin doesn't know either. He told me he just knows somebody on the squad is queer."

"Does Mike Rush know who it is?"

"Does Mike Rush know who it is. I don't know. Yellin didn't say."

"What did Mike Rush offer as evidence that there's a queer on the team?"

"What did Mike Rush offer as evidence," Lloyd said.

"Right."

"I don't know," he said. "But Mike's not the type to make up stories. I know Mike pretty well. Mike's daddy is a committee vice-chairman."

"Look, Lloyd, why are you telling me this?"

"To get your thinking on it, Gary. Yellin and I are getting together in his room later on to figure out what to do. I'm for Kimbrough. Go to Kimbrough with it."

"Because he's one of the captains."

"That's it, that's it. But Yellin wants to go to Dennis Smee. Yellin can't stand Kimbrough. He hates Kimbrough's stinking guts. So he's leaning toward Smee. Maybe even one of the coaches. But I don't think we should go to the coaches at this point. You start with the lower-downs. That's the way it is in anything. Either way we have to figure out what to do and pretty damn soon. There are guys walking around here naked right now. It could be any one of them."

23

I BEGAN TO WORRY seriously about the fact that the
season was nearly over. There would be no more football
until spring practice in April. Without football there was
nothing, really and absolutely nothing, to look forward to.

In class Major Staley lectured on the first-strike survival capability of our nuclear arsenal, ranging from the
land-based Minuteman and Titan missile silos to the nuclear-powered Polaris submarine missile-launching fleet to
the more than five hundred combat-ready bombers of the
Strategic Air Command. There were about forty-five student cadets in Major Staley's class and they were all very
conscientious. But somehow, without even trying, I was by
far the best student in class. I knew the manual almost by
heart and I had read everything the school library had to
offer on aspects of modern war. I asked the most penetrat-
ing questions. I got perfect scores on every quiz. After his
talk on survival capability, the major asked me to remain
after class for a moment. I walked up front and stood by
his desk. He seemed to be looking into my nostrils.

"Gary, you're wasting your time just auditing this
course. You could be getting two credits for it. Join the
cadet wing. It's a good wing. We need your kind of mind
in the wing. Two credits. A meaningful future. The Air
Force is the most self-actualizing branch of the military.
Do one thing for me. Think about joining the wing. Just
think about it. No more, no less."

"The wing," I said. "You want me to join the wing."

"You've got the mind. You've got the good body and the good eyes."

"I don't really, sir, think that I want to go that far in my commitment to this interest I have, seem to have, in the subject matter we've been involved in here. I'm interested in certain areas of this thing in a purely outside interest kind of way. Extracurricular. I don't want to drop H-bombs on the Eskimos or somebody. But I'm not necessarily averse to the purely speculative features of the thing. The hypothetical areas."

"Gary, I'm not asking you to drop bombs on anybody."

"Major, you join an organization like the United States Air Force and before you know it—"

"The leg's been giving me trouble," he said.

"What leg is that, sir?"

"The right leg. I don't know what's the matter with it. I'll have to have it looked at again. They looked at it once before. But I guess they'll have to look again."

"What did they find the first time?"

"Tests were inconclusive."

"You'd better be sure to have it looked at," I said.

"Gary, you've got the seeking-out kind of mind we need in this branch of the service. This arm of the service. Whatever you want to call it."

"I don't know. I don't think so."

"You've got the good eyes. You're an athlete and that's always a plus factor. You've got the body. You've got the probing mind."

"I'm here to play football, major."

"It won't interfere very much. Two hours of drills a week. You're already taking the required classroom work. We've got nine football players in the wing."

"Sir, it's the hypothetical part of it that interests me. I really wouldn't want to get too close to it. I wouldn't want to put on a uniform or anything like that. I wouldn't want to march or visit air bases. I'm interested in certain provinces, areas, and I don't want to get any closer than that. I don't want to get any closer at all."

"Do one thing for me. Think about it. Just think about it. It's a damn good wing for a school this size. Do that for me, Gary. Think about it."

"No," I said.

"You can't say I didn't try. I tried, didn't I?"

"You were very convincing, major. Really, you almost had me there for a minute."

We walked across campus together. I had a class in exobiology coming up and I didn't want to be late. But although I was hurrying right along I had trouble keeping pace with the major. We said good-bye to each other and as he turned to head for the barracks his right leg suddenly buckled and he almost went down. I watched him as he regained his balance and then tried to continue on his way, not looking back at me, limping badly, trying to adjust to the burden of his own weight. I turned and saw Myna Corbett fifty yards ahead. I ran to catch up with her, picking up speed the last ten yards and then coming to an abrupt stop in order to frighten her. It worked beautifully: her startled body was lifted an inch off the ground.

Zapalac circled his desk as he spoke.

"It should be interesting to ask what our life on earth owes to all those comets which deposited so many millions of tons of chemical materials when they crashed into us in the formative years of our history, our growing-up years, and it's probably not too overly poetic to maintain that we were being nourished by the heavens, helped along for our first two billion years or until we could finally do it ourself, synthesize basic materials, take the first step in returning the favor, heading out into space with chow mein dinners fresh from the freezer. But if the truth be known, I'm not really all that fascinated by the carbon content of meteorites or arguing about exactly when the first living organisms appeared on earth. My own feeling is two-seventeen B.C. at Kearney, Nebraska. But what about the last living organisms, the spores and hydrozoans left behind after our protectors protect us into oblivion? We'll all end as astroplankton, clouds of dusty stuff drifting through space. Let me ask. What's the strangest thing about this country? It's that when I wake up tomorrow morning, any morning, the first bit of fear I have doesn't concern our national enemies, our traditional cold-war or whatever-kind-of-war enemies. I'm not afraid of those people at all. So then who am I afraid of because I'm definitely afraid of somebody. Listen and I'll tell you. I'm afraid of my own country. I'm afraid of the United States of America. It's ridiculous, isn't it? But look. Take the Pentagon. If anybody kills us on a grand scale, it'll be the Pentagon. On a small scale, watch out for your local police. Look at you looking at me that way, some of you. Question. Will two polite college-educated-of-course friendly agents of the brainwash squad knock on my door at three in the morning? You see my winning infectious smile and you know I'm not worried. This is America. We say what we want. I could talk all day, citing chapter and verse. But when the true test comes, I'll probably go running to a beauty shop, if you can find one in this neck of the world, and I'll get my hair dyed blond so everybody will think I'm one of those small blondie boys with that faraway look in their eyes who used to be so big on the Himmelplatz three or four decades ago. We're supposed to be talking about biotic potential in today's session as it applies to organisms in far-flung environments, far beyond the highways and byways of our solar system. Man's biotic potential diminishes as everything else increases. That pithy little formula may well earn me a research grant to study modes of survival on the other side of the atmosphere. The first orbiting fellowship. I have a deep thought for you. Science fiction is just beginning to catch up with the Old Testament. See artificial nitrates run off into the rivers and oceans. See carbon dioxide melt the polar ice caps. See the world's mineral reserves dwindle. See war, famine and plague. See barbaric hordes defile the temple of the virgins. See wild stallions mount the prairie dogs. I said science fiction but I guess I meant science. Anyway there's some kind of mythical and/or historic circle-thing being completed here. But I keep smiling. I keep telling myself there's nothing to worry about as long as the youth of America knows what's going on. Brains, brawn, good teeth, tallness. I look at your faces and I have to let out a controversial little grin. Some of you in your nifty blue uniforms here to learn about outer space and how to police it. Uniforms, flags, battle hymns. I offer you my only quotable remark of the entire fall semester. A nation is never more ridiculous than in its patriotic manifestations. Why should I be afraid of my own government? There's something wrong here. But I'm not worried. Fortunately I'm good at ducking. I can bob and weave with the best of them. It takes a lot to stop a little man. Let's open to page seventy-eight. The panspermia hypothesis and its heartwarming implications."

After class Myna invited Zapalac to our picnic that afternoon. I collected my mail and went to my room. Bloomberg was silently asleep, curled about the pillow in a dream. There was a letter in my father's handwriting. It concerned my trip home at Christmastime, still about a month away.

Flying is easy if you keep alert and know what you're doing. When you get to the Midland-Odessa airport, go straight to the ticket counter of the airline you're flying. If the airport there is too small to have separate ticket counters, go to the single all-purpose counter. All right, you're at the counter now. You hand the person the ticket and you put your suitcase on the weight machine. (Carry your ticket in the inside left pocket of your jacket. That's the best place because you're right-handed and you'll be able to reach it easier. It's also safe from anybody with ideas on their mind. They go looking for credit cards to steal mostly. You don't have one yet.) The airline employee will write on your ticket and stamp some things on it purely for airline use and then he'll give you back the ticket and tell you the gate number to go to. Go at once to that gate. If you fool around and start exploring the airport or wandering off somewhere like you always do, you're going to miss your plane. So head for the gate right off the bat and avoid headaches later on. If you have trouble finding the gate, ask someone in authority. That usually means uniformed personnel. When you find the gate, you give your ticket to the man on duty and he sends you aboard the plane. (Your luggage is already on.) Try to get a window seat so you can look out. Don't go to the bathroom until after the plane takes off. Follow similar procedures to the above-mentioned at the Dallas and NYC airports. We'll be at the airport in Saranac Lake to meet you when you land. If there's any foul-up, I'm telling your Aunt Helen where we'll be. So if you don't see us, call your Aunt Helen and she'll know where we are. She's staying home that day on purpose. Don't forget to ask her about her wisdom tooth. And be sure you carry some kind of identification in case of a crash.

For some reason the letter was signed by my mother *(Love, Mom)*. I put it away and got the dictionary. It was time to add a new word to my vocabulary. My word for the day was apotheosis. I looked out the window and repeated to myself the word and its meaning. I used it in three different sentences. I liked the word. It was a particularly beautiful word to be memorizing while looking across the smoldering flannel plain to the tender seam of earth and sky. It was a word lavish with sunlight, with the gods' gladsome songs, the golden power of the sun. I got a blanket and went out to meet Myna.

We ate some fruit and discussed Mexico. She seemed serious about going. She wanted to live in a house that jutted out over a high crag, a house with gardens inside and out. We'd grow our own food, get high whenever we wanted, and read the lives of the saints to each other through the terrifying nights. Zapalac joined us then, loudly, dropping to the blanket as if expecting a sudden burst of small-arms fire. His face split into a warm smile, teeth creamy and even, a filament of spittle fluttering between upper and lower sets.

"I'm glad to be here," he said. "With me it's a constant and never-ending race to get from someplace of no particular distinction to someplace where you were better off before you got there. But this is different. A real, an actual picnic."

"We do it a lot," Myna said. "It's nice to get away, even a few yards."

"This whole place, no exaggeration, is close to unbelievable. From the first day I arrived I figured any minute now the word will go out and everybody will wake up one morning and get out of bed and put on a uniform, an actual military uniform, because everybody will know that the word is out, everybody but me, and they'll see me walking around in my frayed two-button suit that I've worn since high school with moths circling me like vultures ever since and they'll stand me up at a very choice spot against the nearest wall and let me have it. Granted I'm a little bit paranoid. But I've got a nose for terror. I can sense it. I can hear the engines revving. Still, I like it better here than in the Midwest where I was teaching last and where I came across nothing but insanely neat, well-groomed and punctual Republicans. It nearly killed me, the sight of them all, because I get a lift out of, if anything, the confusions, the potential for disorganization in things and people. But my wife is from the Midwest, my wife-to-be if we ever get to see each other again in order to get married, meaning who knows when they'll put on their uniforms and feed me to the dingo dogs out there or whatever they're called, and she's just like the rest of them so I think a certain amount of unpredictability is going to be introduced into her life that she didn't know was lurking on the back steps. Those people know their place. They're masters of the categories of things. They've been raised to believe everything they're told by their elders. They do things in alphabetical order. They know their place. They've known it since early childhood. Drummed into them by respectable parents. The same people who are ripping up the forests with their engines, their money-building machines. But imagine. To respect your elders. It's remarkable, isn't it?"

"I never forget that they're the enemy," Myna said.

"Gary Harkness—is that your name?"

"Right."

"A football player."

"That's right."

"Fantastic," Zapalac said. "What I wouldn't give to be an ace quarterback for the Denver Broncos. I love sports. I love football. I reject the notion of football as warfare. Warfare is warfare. We don't need substitutes because we've got the real thing. Football is discipline. It's team love. It's reason plus passion. The crowds are fantastic. They jump and scream. Hockey, I love hockey. Basketball, too much sweating goes on where you can see it. It's a sweating sport, an armpit sport. But football, I love football. I'm crazy for it. I wallow in it."

"The real needs of man," I said.

"Fantastic," he said.

"Have an orange," Myna said.

"What you were saying earlier about what scares you. Where the true danger is. Something about patriotic manifestations."

"Let me just simply mention flag-waving and the insane repetitive ritualizing that goes on every time a flag is hiked up a pole or some veterans of Gettysburg come hobbling along with their medals, their stickpins, their poppies, their flags, their hats, their banners, their bumper stickers, or some simple sports event where you look up suddenly and there's sixteen thousand Shriners and

Masons with their comical Turkish hats and they're covering every inch of the playing field with, in the middle of them all, three hundred and eighty-five high school girls dressed in red, white and blue who are prostrating themselves on the cold earth as they assume the shape of an American flag being dragged through yak dung by syphilitic foreign students and off to the side there's some crippled television personality in a wheelchair and pulleys singing the national anthem as the cystic fibrosis child of the month poses in the nude for the cover of *Life*. I tend to worry about such spectacles."

"Back in my hometown I took a walk one morning and I kept seeing the same word everywhere I went. Store windows. Leaflets in the street. Advertising space on walls. I kept seeing it for about two weeks. MILITARIZE. It was everywhere—printed, written, scribbled, chalked on walls. I didn't know what it was all about."

"I would have gone into hidding," Zapalac said. "That kind of word, I would have taken food and water and gone into the mountains."

"I would have gone to Mexico," Myna said. "Here, eat this orange, Zap."

"That kind of word, I don't hang around to find out what it all means. I'm a little guy. I look slightly Oriental. I look a little bit Mexican. I've been taken for an Iraqi and I've been taken for a Jew. I don't trust a place where that kind of i-z-e word appears. I-z-e words make me nervous. I go underground. I go into the mountains."

"I'd go running to Canada or Mexico," Myna said. "I'd buy a big house and let everybody stay there who's running away from the i-z-e people. We'd eat chili and nectarines. We'd take care of each other."

"But if you want to know the truth," Zapalac said, "I don't worry about my size at all except as it relates to my inability to gain ace quarterback status with the Denver Broncos. I really want that job. I think about it a lot."

"Size is a big factor," I said.

"Regrettably."

"Tall ~~quarterbacks are in demand because~~ they can peer over the curvature of the earth in order to spot ~~their~~ receivers.

"Fantastic," he said. "From now on, you're my personal bodyguard. When the oilmen and sheriffs form their inevitable posse and come riding after me with thundering hoofbeats, be there in full battle regalia. I've got a class to get to now. Thanks for the orange and try not to be afraid."

Myna ate bean sprouts and drank a can of Afro-Cola. I stuck to fruit. She was wearing her orange dress appliquéd with white atomic mushroom. A beetle moved across the edge of the blanket and I got to my feet and stood off to the side until it was gone. Myna looked at me.

"I hate sudden movements," I said. "It startled me for just a second. I didn't know what it was."

"My brother used to eat them," she said.

"Oh my God."

"Sit down and relax, Gary. Listen to this idea I've got. Vera half-got it, kind of, and I got the rest. It's for your last game. It's a scientific experiment. An audio-visual-sensory-type thing."

"What is it?"

"Smoke some dope before the game."

"They'd kill me."

"Tell what's-his-thing not to give you the ball. The big jerk. The one who calls the plays."

"Hobbs."

"Tell him not to give you the ball. You could just stand off to the side and observe what it all looks like. I bet it would look wild, Gary. All that running and the colors. Would it be speeded up or slowed down? Would your sensory parts function in terms of football or dope? You wouldn't have to carry the ball."

"Ball or no ball, I'd get killed. I'd have no coordination. I'd just stand there and get hit. They'd kill me. They'd tear me to pieces."

"I guess you're right. It's better not to take chances.

But it would have been tremendous to observe all that action from close up and being high."

"There's no tension in our relationship," I said.

"Where did that come from? What do you mean? Now don't talk that way, Gary. You know the way I am when it comes to us. I'm too emotional to just sit here and talk about our relationship. That's a horrible word anyway."

"I was just fooling around. Probing for a sense of definition. How's your book coming along?"

"This book is an unbelievable book. I don't know what else to say. Do you want to hear what it's all about?"

"I don't think so."

"It's the last part of a trilogy by Tudev Nemkhu, that Mongolian I mentioned once before. It's a whole total experience, Gary. I'll just tell you one or two little things about it."

"How little?"

"These half-mollusk creatures called nautiloids inhabit a tiny planet in a galaxy not too far from here. The planet has just one ocean. It's a big round circle of liquid and gases. That's where the nautiloids live. The rest of the planet is barren except for one small mountain. There's no surface life whatsoever. There's just the nautiloids in the ocean. The nautiloids, who are about twice human-size, communicate with each other through some intricate ESP number system that the author spends almost two chapters on but that's way over my head but still tremendous to read if only because it kills me to think how anybody could think of this thing. I forgot to tell you, Gary. There's a thick hard foam that encases the planet about fifty miles above the surface. So anyway one day without warning there's a disturbance in the nautiloids' system of communication. Their numerical language gets all garbled. They can't communicate properly and they get very disoriented and panic-stricken. Some of them start coming up out of the ocean. Then more of them come up. They crawl over the land. They're all in a state of panic. Then one of them goes into a fantastic spasm and breaks out of its shell. At the very second this happens, the thick foam around the planet also breaks. Then there's silence everywhere. Oh, I forgot to tell you. The mountain is completely uneroded. It's triangular in shape. And because of its strange configuration, if you were to walk completely around it you would always see the same flat plane in the shape of a triangle. So the nautiloids go back to the ocean. All but the one that broke out of its shell. It stays there on the ground until finally something comes pouring through the break in the planet's outer crust. It's powdery black light. It's a form of electromagnetic radiation that's semi-black and has weird texture. The author spends dozens of pages on this part. So then the light becomes sort of infused into the complex brain apparatus of the nautiloid. The creature's form begins to change. The black light continues to wash over the creature for what we would call many centuries but what in cosmic terms is just an eyelash blinking. The creature's body becomes incredible. Tudev Nemkhu almost doesn't even want to describe it. Finally he does it but only in terms of chemical formulas, mathematical equations and statements from formal logic which I think are all supposed to be really true and documented and not just made up. So there's this creature that's been formed of the landscape itself through the power of this black light. It's almost an abstract being. It's barren of features or really of any kind of distinguishing elements. I guess it's hard for people with arms and legs to conceive of this thing. The thing is visible but not really describable except in scientific terms. But it's not just a blob or a bunch of protons. It's a mass of equations and formulas rendered into some kind of tangible form. The thing's shape changes a million times every millionth of a second. That gives you some idea. And its brain is slowly evolving into phases of light and nonlight."

"What does that mean?"

"I don't know," she said. "But then everything begins to double. Within the thing's brain mechanism there are now two landscapes perceived by two mechanisms. The thing sees itself seeing what is outside it being seen by itself. As Tudev Nemkhu explains it, this duplication results in the making of words. Each likeness is a word rather than a thing. When the word is imprinted on the thing's original mechanism, the likeness that was the word's picture instantaneously disappears. The thing's brain keeps on producing likenesses and then delivering words into its own circuitry. The thing perceives everything into itself. It duplicates perceptions and then reduplicates the results. The author finally gives the thing a name. The thing becomes monadanom—the thing that's everything. It keeps making likenesses to make words. The words have no meaning. They're just fragments of cosmic language. So everything is existing inside this complex brain apparatus that was formerly based on a numerical system and that now is guided by phases of light and nonlight, or something pretty much like that. And this duplication goes on and on for what we would call millenniums until suddenly without warning one of the words erases itself. The brain didn't order this and doesn't comprehend it. The word just erased itself. It no longer exists. There is no record of it."

"What about the triangular mountain?" I said.

"That's as far as I've gotten. I guess the mountain turns up again in the ending. I forgot to tell you one other thing. The thick foam around the planet is an organic self-healing thing. The crack is slowly closing up again."

"Monadanom," I said.

"That right."

"And this guy's a Mongolian."

"That's right, Gary. But he writes in German instead of Mongol. The translation leaves a lot to be desired. Which reminds me. Vera wants a sample of your handwriting."

"What for?"

"Vera's into psychographology and character analysis.

It's all related to early Mayan forms of astrology. Esther's into bottled water."

"I just thought of something," I said.

"What, Gary?"

"That word I kept seeing all over town. It represented some kind of apotheosis. I'm pretty sure that's what it was. An apotheosis of some kind. The air was thick with it."

24

I STUCK MY HEAD under the black windbreaker that hung inside my dressing cubicle in the locker room. Then I took two more drags on the joint, whistling in reverse, swallowing deeply, all vigilance and greed. Two more drags then. My throat was very dry; it burned a bit. I stepped back away from the cubicle, hoping all stray smoke would cling to the garments hanging there. I wondered if my teammates or the coaches could smell anything or detect visually a trace of modest smog. The place was getting quieter. We were almost ready to take the field. I was all suited up except for headgear. I palmed the joint and went quickly into the bathroom. In one of the stalls somebody was trying to vomit. It was a poignant sound, monumentally hoarse, soulful, oddly lacking in urgency. A herd of seals. I entered the far stall and tried another drag. The pinpoint glow was gone already but I had a book of matches tucked into one of my shoes. I lit up again and inhaled deeply, getting paper and loose grains along with the smoke. I took in everything, hurrying, feeling the smoke pinch my sensitive palpitating throat, watching the remaining paper sputter slightly and go brown, then dragging again and lip-breathing like a malevolent jungle plant to gather in the escaping smoke and finally sucking everything into the deepest parts of my lungs and brain. The sick player emerged. I peered out at him from a narrow opening as he washed up and gargled with cold water. It was 47, Bobby Hopper. I took a final drag, then flushed butt-end and matches down the toilet; there would be no safe way to use them later on. Bobby and I left the bathroom together. Mitchell Gorse passed us on his way to throw up.

I drank some water from the fountain, swallowed, then took another mouthful and spat it on the concrete floor. I liked to spit water all over the floor. It was something you couldn't do indoors as a rule. In a few minutes we were out on the field. Some kind of ceremony was going on. I sat on the bench waiting for the game to start. It was a cool bright afternoon. The grass seemed extremely green. Buddy Shock came over, put one foot on the bench and leaned toward me.

"Gary, we didn't hit each other. We didn't trade blows. You didn't give me the forearm to the chest. I looked all over for you."

"Not today, Buddy."

"It's a tradition. We have to do it. It'll be bad luck not to do it. Come on, get up, I want to put three dents in your head."

"I don't plan any quick movements just yet. I'm saving myself. It's a new methodology I've just worked out."

"We've done it eight games running, Gary."

"When men vomit together, they feel joined in body and spirit. Women have no such luck."

"I hate to see a good tradition wiped out," Buddy said.

In a little while the ceremony ended. I was feeling heavy-headed; the air was getting thick. Bing Jackmin kicked off. The opposition sustained a drive for three first downs, about eight plays, before losing the ball on a fumble. As I started out I felt unbelievably ponderous. My head was made of Aztec stone. I watched my feet go slowly up and down over the marvelous grass. My teammates were out there already, waiting for me. Garland Hobbs stood above the huddle, above the lowered heads, waiting for me to get there. I continued across the grass, uncranking my arms, watching the long white laces whisk lightly over my black shoes. I reached the huddle. I realized I didn't want to be with all these people. They were all staring at me through their cages. Hobbs called a pass play. We broke and set. Somebody came at me, a huge individual in silver and blue. I fell at his feet and grabbed one shoe. I started untying the lace. He kicked away from me and went after Hobbs. I got up and walked off. I was exceedingly hungry.

The next day Terry Madden and I were playing gin rummy in the lounge. Link Brownlee dragged a chair over and sat down.

"Did you hear?" he said.

"What?" I said.

"Taft Robinson. You haven't seen him? You haven't heard?"

"No, what?"

"He shaved his skull. He's bald."

"How bald?" Terry said.

"Completely and totally bald. He shaved his skull. He must have done it last night."

"What do you think it means?" Terry said.

"I don't know," I said. "I don't know what it means. How would I know what it means?"

"It means something," he said.

"Thing used to be so simple," Brownlee said.

25

WALLY PIPPICH SAT behind his desk, facing up into a sun lamp, a strip of Reynolds Wrap covering his eyes. The smell of mops standing in dirty water had penetrated the office.

"Gary, I called you in here to get briefed on the so-called leaving the game incident. I was downstate doing advance work on an all-girl rodeo so I've had to rely on eyewitness accounts. As it was given to me, word for word, you walked right off the field after your team's first play from scrimmage. Everybody thought you were injured."

"I was hungry," I said.

"That's what I understand your story is. The story you told Oscar Veech. That's what you allege to be the case. Hunger pangs."

"I just couldn't stay out there. I was really starved for something to eat. Hunger pangs can be interpreted as a form of injury. I had to leave and get some food."

I liked the idea of talking with someone who could not see me. I watched his mouth as he spoke. It was extremely active, almost an animated cartoon, a visual guide to the soundmaking process. His mouth seemed to invent the words as well as speak them; it was as though he'd been raised among lip readers. Wally's tongue was lumpy and bluish. His right hand, hanging down between his thighs, moved in a vaguely masturbatory way as he spoke.

"The game had just started," he said. "Oscar Veech said he saw you fall on the ground and grab somebody's foot. He thought you were sick or having some kind of fit."

"I was hungry. Really, that's all it was."

"Gary, I'm going to level with you. I don't believe a word you're saying. Nobody leaves an intercollegiate athletic event out of sheer appetite motivations."

"Wally, why else? Why else then? Why would I walk off like that?"

"I know one thing, Gary. You've piqued my innate curiosity. This kind of thing is bread and butter to me. This is part and parcel of the dream stuff of publicity and public relations. I want to follow up on this thing. I'd like to see what I can do with it. Temperamental star. Psychosis attack. Loss of memory. Give me something to go on. I'll slam out a human interest thing, real fast, down and dirty, and I'll get it to the wire services for immediate release. Season's over. We have to get moving on it."

"What are they going to do to me?" I said.

"They can't suspend you because there aren't any games left. And I don't know what Emmett thinks because he's under the weather. They've got him isolated over in his room. I guess they'll just have to wait on Emmett."

"We won the game," I said. "I knew there wouldn't be any problem. I wouldn't have left if I thought we'd have trouble winning."

"Gary, I've told you all I know. I'll stick my neck out for you if the situation calls for any necks to be stuck out. In return I ask just one thing. Tell me what happened. Tell me why you walked off the field."

"I had to make peepee."

"Pissation."

"That's right."

"Gary, I like flair. I like freak appeal. I like any kind of charisma. When I was an access coordinator for the phone company, I got together a specialty act in my spare time. Two sword-swallowers on a trampoline. You got to daze people. You got to climb inside their mouth. Gary, I'll stick up for you all the way. Next season we make it big. The T and G backfield. I sure do like the sound of that. Slick as a turd."

"Wally, aren't you going to hurt your eyes with just that aluminum foil over them?"

"This stuff is oven-tempered," he said.

I took a long walk around the college grounds. The wind blew across the plains, gusting now, leaving gray dust everywhere, on buildings, trees, benches, so that in time we too seemed bare, the campus and its people, sparse as the land around us, the hand of the wind on everything. I walked back to Staley Hall. In my room I did nothing for an hour or more. Then I went to visit Billy Mast. He was sitting on his bed, sewing a button on a blue dress. Ted Joost walked in behind me. He and I talked about Billy's course in the untellable. Billy himself merely listened. In a few minutes, Chester Randall and Jeff Elliott came in. Chester wore an old bathrobe and basketball sneakers.

"Nothing's happening," he said. "I've been walking the halls all afternoon. I've been trying to figure out what might be happening. Season's over. Nothing's happening."

"I tried to get in to see Coach," Jeff said. "But he can't see anybody yet."

"Whose dress is that?" Chester said.

Chuck Deering walked in. He did a dance step and then went over and sat on the windowsill.

"Whose dress is that?" he said. "Is that Alla Joy Burney's dress? Let me put my head in there. I want to bury my head in that erotic material."

"We might as well take turns," Chester said. "There's no reason not to, what with the season being over. Nothing happening till spring practice."

"I graduate," Deering said. "Talk about nothing happening, that's the biggest nothing there is. That's the ultimate nothing. I graduate in the spring."

"No more football," Billy Mast said.

"I'm all through school. I graduate. I'm gone for good."

"No more football. No more hitting. No more sweat and pain. No more fear."

"I can't believe it."

"No more being yelled at and cursed by those insane coaches. No more running in the heat. No more two laps around the goal posts. No more getting kicked and elbowed and spat upon."

"It's awful. I can't accept it. It's a bitch."

"Literally spat upon," Billy said. "No more. None of it. Never. Not ever again for the rest of your natural days."

"I need the dress. Give me the dress. I have to put my head under the dress."

Bobby Iselin and Bobby Hopper came in. Iselin was still limping from the Centrex game.

"Did you hear?" Hopper said. "Mrs. Tom was in a plane crash. She was in a light plane going to some conference. It overshot the runway. She's on the critical list."

"Let's have the details," Jeff said.

"Those *are* the details. I about wet my pants when I heard."

"Let me get it straight. Critical list. Overshot the runway. Light plane."

"Going to some conference."

"Look at that dress," Bobby Iselin said. "Whose dress is that? I bet that's Alla Joy Burney's dress."

"He won't let me put my head under it," Deering said.

"That's about the only exercise we can expect to get," Chester said. "I've been walking the halls all afternoon. One thought in mind. Spring practice. We hit and get hit. We sweat off the excess poundage. We really sweat. Sweeee-et. We hit. We hurl our bodies. We get hit."

"Not Deering," Jeff said.

"Not me. I've had it forever. I graduate. I'm gone for

good. The ultimate nothing. My only hope is Billy gives me some leeway with that damn dress."

George Dole walked in.

"They got Coach behind closed doors," he said. "They're keeping him isolated for some reason."

"Did you hear about the plane crash?" Jeff said. "She's on the critical list. It overshot the runway. She was in a light plane going to some conference. Bobby knows the details."

"Who's on the critical list?"

"Mrs. Tom," Hopper said. "It overshot the runway. She's on the critical list. I'd prefer to be called Bob from now on. I'll be a senior next year. I've had it with Bobby."

"That's a damn shame. No, I didn't hear about that. I didn't know about that at all. This is the first I've heard."

Howard Lowry, Billy's roommate, came in and sat on the desk, addressing himself to Billy.

"People keep bringing up that course you're taking. The untellable. I keep hearing about that course. Nobody talks about it but I keep hearing."

"So do I," Ted Joost said.

"There's not much I can say about it," Billy said.

"You can tell us what goes on."

"We delve into the untellable."

"How deep?" Bobby Iselin said.

"It's hard to tell. I don't think anybody knows how deep the untellable is. We've done a certain amount of delving. We plan to delve some more. That's about all I can tell you."

"But what do you talk about?" Howard said. "There are ten of you in there and there's some kind of instructor or professor. You must say things to each other."

"We shout in German a lot. There are different language exercises we take turns doing. We may go on a field trip next week. I don't know where to."

"But you don't know German. I know damn well you

don't. I'm your damn roommate. I know things about you."

"Unfortunately I've picked up a few words. I guess that's one of the hazards in a course like this. You pick up things you're better off without. The course is pretty experimental. It's given by a man who may or may not have spent three and a half years in one of the camps. He doesn't think there'll be a final exam."

"Why things in German?" Ted Joost said.

"I think the theory is if any words exist beyond speech, they're probably German words, or pretty close."

"What do I say to people who keep bringing up the untellable?" Howard said.

"It's a three-credit course. It's a very hard course, no matter how bright you are. And apparently there are field trips. I don't know what else you can tell them."

"Look at him work on that dress," Deering said. "Let me at least lick the button before you finish sewing it. That's all I ask. If I can't put my head under the dress, at least let me lick the button."

"I really and truly did not know about the plane crash at all," George said. "It overshot the runway. Is that what happened?"

"They had to rush her to the hospital," Hopper said.

"Did she regain consciousness?"

"I don't know if she ever lost it. I just know they had to rush her to the hospital. She's on the critical list."

Tim Flanders and John Butler came in. Butler carried a laundry bag and three pairs of sneakers.

"Did you hear about the plane crash?" George said.

"We just heard," Buttler said.

"She was in a light plane going to some conference. It overshot the runway. She's on the critical list."

"It overshot the runway. That's what we heard."

"They had to rush her to the hospital."

"I wonder if it was raining," Flanders said. "Usually they overshoot in bad weather."

"We don't have anything on that yet," Hopper said.

"We don't know if she lost or regained consciousness either. I about wet my pants when I heard."

"A lot of times they die without regaining consciousness," Chester said.

"I wonder if she was burned beyond recognition," Flanders said. "That usually happens in that kind of crash."

John Jessup appeared in the doorway.

"What kind of news you got for us?" Jeff said.

"Shit-news."

"Can you give us any details?"

"Chudko has the details. Chudko has all the particulars. I just know it's shit-news. Anybody wants details, go hunt up Chudko."

"Whose dress is that?" Butler said. "That must be Alla Joy Burney's dress. Hey, move over, Bobby. Plenty of room."

"I get first crack at that dress," Deering said. "There's a waiting line for that dress. My head goes under first."

"I don't know how people can chew just one stick of gum," George Dole said. "I chew all five."

Billy Mast re-threaded the needle, somewhat theatrically. Spurgeon Cole, Jerry Fallon and Dickie Kidd walked in. It was getting dark outside. I heard the wind rip around the building, actually turning corners, sounding wild enough to unpile stone. John Butler and Bobby Hopper started fighting for some reason. Several good punches were thrown. Then Randy King came in, swinging between a pair of crutches. He was wearing his team jersey, number 51.

26

IN THE DARKNESS I listened to Bloomberg tapping the wall next to his bed. I turned the other way, toward my own wall, and tried to fall asleep. I reviewed the entire day. I reviewed the week just past. I tried to remember the precise meaning of a certain phrase: interval recognition bombing. Nothing helped. I remained wide awake. Seven feet away the tapping continued, the thin steady click of fingernails, of penitentiary teaspoons. In time he switched to knuckles.

"Anatole."

"What is it?"

"This isn't Devil's Island. If you want to communicate with the people next door, you're free to walk right in."

"What do you mean?"

"You were tapping," I said.

"Was I tapping? Was I hitting the wall? I'm sorry, Gary. I didn't know."

"It's all right."

"Was I keeping you awake? I'm really sorry. I didn't know I was doing it."

"It's all right, Anatole. Really. I just thought I'd mention it. In fact, if you want to keep tapping, if it helps you fall asleep or even if it just reduces tension, go right ahead. It doesn't bother me all that much."

"What was I tapping with?" he said.

"Your hand."

"What part?"

"I think it was fingernails first, then knuckles."

"That reverses the pattern," he said. "I used to tap all the time when I was a child. But I always started out with knuckles. This reverses the pattern."

Although it was too dark to see anything, I rolled over in order to be facing him while we spoke.

"Why did you tap as a child, Anatole?"

"Children do that sort of thing. Probe everywhere for magic. There was always the chance somebody might answer."

"Did anybody ever answer?"

"There was a warehouse on the other side of the wall. Nobody ever answered. But one night, as I was just getting into bed, I heard a sound from the wall. I started tapping. I tapped for at least half an hour. I tried to improvise codes. I tried to convey urgency by using both hands to tap. There was no reply. It was probably a rat."

"Did this have some kind of effect on you, do you think?"

"It had no effect at all. What kind of effect would it have? It had a ridiculous effect. I was tapping at rats. That's the only effect."

"But why were you tapping so urgently, do you think?"

"I wanted to be sure the sound knew I was there. I didn't know what kind of hearing the sound possessed. It occurred to me that the sound might possess a very primitive hearing apparatus. I wanted to impress on it the fact that there was somebody on the other side of the wall. The sound might have been anything. I felt this was not the time to be subtle. I wanted to be sure the sound heard me."

"Why were you tapping a few minutes ago?" I said. "Had you heard a sound?"

"I didn't know I was tapping. I have only your word for it. I guess it was some kind of locomotor memory retrogression. As you know, I also wet the bed."

"But not nearly as much as you used to."

"Just as much but not as often," he said. "The improvement, obviously, is due to my recent efforts to forge a new consciousness."

"Right," I said. "A sort of new man kind of thing. The new man. The nonethnic superrational man. That kind of thing, right?"

"That's about right, Gary."

"Your phrasing gets more precise every day. I've been noticing that."

"I try to speak in complete sentences at least ninety-five percent of the time. Subject, predicate, object. It's a way of escaping the smelly undisciplined past with all its ridiculous customs and all its craziness—centuries of middle-European anxiety and guilt. I want to think clearly. I train myself toward that end with every living fiber of my being."

"Anatole, forgive me but that seems a little bit simplistic. Speak straight and you'll think straight."

"There's a relatedness. Take my word."

"Where did you grow up?" I said. "I've always been reluctant to ask."

"I don't want to discuss that. It no longer has any relevance. It's excess baggage. I'm getting rid of it. Go to sleep now, Gary, and try not to snore."

"Do you plan eventually to change your name?"

"There's no need for that. I've already reached the point where my name connotes nothing more to me than the designation EK-seventeen might connote. I don't feel I have to live up to my name, to defend it, to like it, to spell it. I used to think of Anatole Bloomberg as the essence of European Jewry. I used to think I had to live up to my name. I thought I had to become Anatole Bloomberg, an importer-exporter from Rotterdam with a hook nose and flat feet, or an Antwerp diamond merchant wearing a skull-cap, or a hunchbacked Talmudic scholar in a woolly black coat and shoes without shoelaces. Those are just three of the autobiographical projections I had to contend with. It was my name that caused the trouble, the Europeness of my name. Its Europicity. And there was another thing. Some names possess a smell. I didn't like the way my name smelled. It was like a hallway in a tenement where a lot of Bulgarians live. But that's all over now. Now I'm free. I'm EK-seventeen."

"It's a fabulous name," I said. "I mean the original one. I'm glad you're keeping it."

"It's a means of identification. It has no significance beyond that."

"Good night, Anatole."

"When I arrived here last year," he said, "I was still in a state of confusion and inner panic. But the remoteness helped me. The desert was an ideal place in which to begin the process of unjewing. I spoke aloud to myself in the desert, straightening out my grammar, getting rid of the old slang and the old speech rhythms. I walked in straight lines. I tried to line myself up parallel to the horizon and then walk in a perfectly straight line. I tried to become single-minded and straightforward, to keep my mind set on one thought or problem until I was finished with it. It was hot and lonely. I wore a lot of clothing to keep the sun from burning me and causing my skin to peel. Sometimes I read aloud from a children's reader. I wanted to start all over with simple declarative sentences. Subject, predicate, object. Dick opened the door. Jane fed the dog. It helped me immensely. I began to think more clearly, to concentrate, to leave behind the old words and aromas and guilts. Then I was called to the telephone. My mother had been shot to death by a lunatic. It all came back, who I was, what I was, where the past crossed over into the present and from being to being. Another innocent victim. I didn't go home to look at her small dead body. That would have been too much of a bringing back. I was sure I would never recover from the unspeakable heartbreak and Jewishness of her funeral. So I didn't go home."

Instead I went into the desert with a paintbrush and a can of black paint. Among all those flat stones I found a single round one. I painted it black. It's my mother's burial marker."

27

IT RAINED AND THEN SNOWED. I wrote letters through the blurred afternoons, embryonic queries on the nature of silence and time, notes really, laconic and hopeful, ready for bottling, and I mailed them to friends and former teachers, to people back home, to self-possessed young women in prospering colleges. There were no picnics with Myna. The days seemed even longer than the incandescent days of summer. Mrs. Tom died finally after remaining in a coma for several weeks.

I took a walk down the hall and dropped into Taft's room. He was sitting on his bed, legs bent in, back quite straight, reading a huge gray book. I sat by his desk. Beyond the window was that other world, unsyllabled, snow lifted in the wind, swirling up, massing within the lightless white day, falling toward the sky. The blanket was gray. The walls were bare except for an inch of transparent tape curling into itself, thumb-smudged, just one corner sticking now, a small light imprint on the wall indicating (to anyone who was interested) exactly how the tape had first been applied, at what angle to the ceiling, at what approximate angle to the intersection of that wall with each adjacent wall, at what angle to all other fixed lines in the room. The complete and absolute bareness of the walls (tapeless) made the tape seem historic. This room had not existed one year before. Room and building were new. Tape was (most likely) almost as old as the room itself, judged by poor coloring and generally shriveled appearance. Tape therefore (applied) was as old as the man occupying the room in terms of room-age or the lapsed-time-occupancy factor. Tape and man had a special relationship. (As did room and man, tape and room.) They were coeval, in room-time, and existed as the sum of a number of varying angles. I yawned and rubbed my eyes, bored with myself. Both my shoelaces were untied. Taft went on reading, his head bowed slightly. I studied the topography of his skull, searching for mountain ranges and rivers, for a sign of ancient civilizations under the saltwhite sand. Without hair, I thought, you will run even faster. Vision of a torchbearer black in the high dawn of a mountain country. (Spurgeon Cole stood beneath the goal posts, repeating them, arms raised in the shape of a crossbar and uprights, his fists clenched. The crowd was still up, leaning, in full voice, addressing its own noise. This was it then, the legend, the beauty, the mystery of black speed. Perhaps twenty thousand people watched, overjoyed to see it finally, to partake in the ceremony of speed, in statistical prayer, the human effort tracked by pulsing lights. They were privileged to witness what happened in real time, nonelectronically, in that obscure compass point of America, all standing now, the young men of boot-camp countenance, the light-haired girls with freckled arms, the men with sheriff bellies, the bespectacled and long-necked women—crafty grim inedible birds—of middle age, the old men with one shoulder higher than the other, with dented felt hats and stained teeth. It was not just the run that had brought them to their feet; it was the idea of the run, the history of it. Taft's speed had a life and history of its own, independent of him. To wonder at this past. To understand the speed, that it was something unknown to them, never to be known. Hip-width. Leg-length. Tendon and tibia. Hyperextensibility. But more too: wizardry drawn from wells in black buckets. Much to consider that could not be measured in simple centimeters. Strange that this demon speed could be distilled from the doldrums of old lands. But at least they had seen it now. The hawks in their lonesome sky. It had been a sight to ease the greed of all sporting souls. Maybe they had loved him in those few raw seconds. Truly loved him in the dark art of his speed. That was the far reach of the moment, their difficult love for magic.) Taft wore a white shirt and gray pants. His socks were black. I wondered if he had planned to put a poster on the wall and if he had then changed his mind, stripping off all but one piece of tape. What kind of poster, I thought. Of what or whom. It would have told something. That, I knew, was why he hadn't put it up. And now he enveloped his presence in neutral shades. (A somber cream covered the walls and ceiling.) In his austerity he blended with the shadowless room, reading his gray history, a dreamer of facts. Everywhere it was possible to perceive varieties of silence, small pauses in corners, rectangular planes of stillness, the insides of desks and closets (where shoes curl in dust), the spaces between things, the endless silence of surfaces, time swallowed by methodically silent clocks, whispering air and the speechlessness of sentient beings, all these broken codes contained in the surrounding calm, the vastness beyond the window, sunblaze, a clash of metals no louder than heat on flesh. The snow had stopped falling. I got up and went back to my room.

28

JIM DEERING BROUGHT a football out to the parade grounds and we played for several hours in the fresh snow. It began as a game of touch, five on a side, no contact except for brush blocks and tagging the ballcarrier. The snow was ankle-high. We let the large men do all the throwing. Some of us cut classes in order to keep playing. It was very cold at first but we didn't notice so much after a while. Nobody cared how many passes were dropped or badly thrown and it didn't matter how slowly we ran or if we fell trying to cut or stop short. The idea was to keep playing, keep moving, get it going again. Some students and teachers, walking to and from classes, stood and watched for a few minutes and then went away. Two more players entered the game, making it six to a side. They left their books on top of the pile of heavy coats in the snow. Most of us wore regular shoes and nothing heavier than a sweater. George Dole, his first chance to play quarterback, wore a checkered cowboy shirt with the sleeves rolled way up. Nobody wore gloves after John Jessup said gloves were outlawed. Toward the end of the first hour it began getting windy. The wind blew loose snow into our faces, making it hard to keep track of the ball's flight. Between plays I crossed my arms over my chest, keeping my hands wedged in my armpits for warmth. We blocked a little more emphatically now, partly to keep warm, to increase movement, and also to compensate for the wind, the poor playing conditions; more hitting helped us forget the sting of cold snow blowing in our faces. Each team had just one deep back to do all the throwing and running; there were three linemen blocking and two receivers. Defense was a 3–3 most of the time. It was getting harder to complete a pass or turn the corner on a running play. I noticed that Buddy Shock's nose was bleeding. It started to snow now, lightly at first, then more heavily, and in time it was almost impossible to see beyond the limits of the parade grounds. It was lovely to be hemmed in that way, everything white except for the clothes we wore and the football and the bundle of coats and books in the snow nearby. We were part of the weather, right inside it, isolated from objects on the land, from land, from perspective itself. There were no spectators now; we were totally alone. I was beginning to enjoy skidding and falling. I didn't even try to retain my balance when I felt myself slipping. Certain reflexes were kept slack; it seemed fitting to let the conditions determine how our bodies behaved. We were adrift within this time and place and what I experienced then, speaking just for myself, was some variety of environmental bliss. Jessup outlawed the placing of hands under armpits between plays. I found merit in this regulation; even the smallest warmth compromised immersion in the elements. Then he outlawed huddles and the making of plays in the usual way. Each play, he decreed, would be announced aloud by the team with the ball. There would be no surprise at all, not the slightest deception; the defense would know exactly what was coming. Again I found it easy to agree. We were getting extremely basic, moving into elemental realms, seeking harmony with the weather and the earth. The snowfall was very heavy now, reducing visibility to about fifteen yards. Suddenly Tim Flanders and Larry Nix were standing near the coats. Someone had told them about the game and they had come down hoping to get in. That made it seven men on each team, four blockers, an unbalanced line, a 4–3 defense. I was playing center now, stooped way over, my body warped and about to buckle, hands positioned on the cold wet ball, eyes on huge George Dole awaiting the snap four yards behind me and upside-down, calling out the play and number, his face that of an outlandishly large Navaho infant, dull muddy red in color, his feet lost in snow, sniffling now as he shouted out the cadence, white haired in the biting wind, abominable and looming. The blocking became more spirited and since we wore no equipment it was inevitable that tempers would flare. Randall and Nix butted each other a few times, throwing no punches because of the severe cold. Then Jessup outlawed passing plays. It became strictly a ground game. After two plays it was decided, by unanimous consent, to replace tagging with tackling. Naturally the amount of hitting increased. Somebody tore my sweater and left me buried in snow. I got up and kept going. With passing outlawed the game changed completely. Its range was now limited to a very small area and its degree of specialization diminished. There were no receivers and defenders to scatter the action. We were all blockers, all tacklers. Only the ball-carrier, one man, could attempt to use evasion and finesse in avoiding the primal impact. After a clumsy double-reverse I stood alone watching Ron Steeples, way over at the far rim of vision, whirl in a rotary cloud of snow and take a swing at Jim Deering, whose back was turned. Steeples lost his balance as he swung; the punch missed completely and he fell. Deering, unaware of any of this, trotted over to his side of the line. Steeples got up and walked slowly toward the defense, wiping his hands on his stiff wet trousers. At this point Jessup banned reverses of any kind. The ball had to be handled by one man and one man alone. Even fake reverses were outlawed. No offensive player could pass in front of or behind the ball-carrier while the ballcarrier was still behind the line of scrimmage. Jessup shouted these regulations into the wind. I asked about laterals. Absolutely forbidden, Jessup said. My hands were numb. I looked at them. They were purplish red. Snow on my lashes blurred everything. Lines of sight shortened. My shoes weighed me down. We kept playing, we kept hitting, and we were comforted by the noise and brunt of our bodies in contact, by the simple physical warmth generated through violent action, by the sight of each other, the torn clothing, the bruises and scratches, the wildness of all fourteen, numb, purple, coughing, white heads solemn in the healing snow. Jessup banned end runs. It became a straight-ahead game, tackle to tackle. We hand-fought and butted. Linemen fired out and the ballcarrier just lowered his head and went pounding into the tense rhythmic mass. Blocking did not necessarily cease when the ballcarrier went down. Private battles continued until one man gave ground or was buried in snow. These individual contests raged on every play, each man grunting and panting, trying to maintain traction, to move the other man, to chop him down, to overwhelm him. Randall grabbed me by the shoulders and tried to toss me off to the side. I slipped out of his grip, getting hit on the back of the neck with a stray elbow, and then I rammed a shoulder into his gut and kept on moving, kept driving, making him give way; but he tightened up, hardening considerably now, too strong for me, coming back with a slap to my left ear which turned me half-around and then moving straight in with everything, head, shoulders, hands, until he buried me. He dug me out and slapped me on the rump. On the next play I cross-blocked, going after Deering, more my size, standing him up with two shoulder-blows to the chest, getting shoved from behind and going down with three or four others. The cold was painful now; it hurt more than the blocking and tackling. I got up, one shoe missing. I saw it a few yards away. I went over and picked it up. It felt like a dead animal. I forced it over my foot. The laces were stiff and my hands too frozen to make a knot. I looked up. Oscar Veech was standing directly in front of me, wearing a padded ski jacket and a pair of snow goggles.

"Coach wants to see you," he said.

Everybody stood around watching. I went over and

found my coat. I put it over my head and followed Veech into the dimness and silence. We went over to Staley Hall. Veech didn't say anything. We went downstairs and he simply nodded toward the closed door at the end of the isometrics room. I left my coat bundled on a scale. Then I blew my nose, walked to the door and knocked. The room was small and barely furnished, just an army cot, a small folding table, two folding chairs. There were no windows. On the wall was a page torn from a book, a black-and-white plate of a girl praying in a medieval cell, an upper corner of the page loose and casting a limp shadow. Near the door, at my shoulder, a whistle hung from a string looped over a bent nail. Emmett Creed was in a wheelchair. His legs were covered with a heavy blanket, gray and white, not quite the school colors. Ten or twelve loose-leaf binders were stacked neatly on the floor.

"Sit down, Gary."

"Yes sir."

"I'm told it's a near blizzard out there."

"We were going at it," I said. "We were playing. We were ignoring the weather and going right at it."

"So I'm told."

"How are you feeling, Coach? A lot of the guys have tried to get in to see you. I'm sure they'd appreciate it if I brought back word."

"Everything is progressing as anticipated."

"Yes sir. Very good. I know they'd appreciate hearing that."

"A near blizzard is what they tell me."

"It's really snowing," I said. "It's coming down thick and steady. Visibility must be zero feet."

"Maybe that's the kind of weather we needed over at Centrex."

"None of us can forget that game, Coach."

"We learned a lot of humility on that field."

"It was hard to accept. We had worked too hard to lose, going all the way back to last summer, scrimmaging in that heat. We had worked too hard. It was impossible to believe that anybody had worked harder than we had. We had sacrificed. We had put ourselves through a series of really strenuous ordeals. And then to step out on that field and be overwhelmed the way we were."

"It takes character to win," he said. "It's not just the amount of mileage you put in. The insults to the body. The humiliation and fear. It's dedication, it's character, it's pride. We've got a ways to go yet before we develop these qualities on a team basis."

"Yes sir."

"I've never seen a good football player who didn't know the value of self-sacrifice."

"Yes sir."

"I've never seen a good football player who wanted to learn a foreign language."

"Yes."

"I've been married three times but I was never blessed with children. A son. So maybe I don't know as much about young men as I think I do. But I've managed to get some good results through the years. I've tried to extract the maximal effort from every boy I've ever coached. Or near as possible. Football is a complex of systems. It's like no other sport. When the game is played properly, it's an interlocking of a number of systems. The individual. The small cluster he's part of. The larger unit, the eleven. People stress the violence. That's the smallest part of it. Football is brutal only from a distance. In the middle of it there's a calm, a tranquillity. The players accept pain. There's a sense of order even at the end of a running play with bodies strewn everywhere. When the systems interlock, there's a satisfaction to the game that can't be duplicated. There's a harmony."

"Absolutely," I said.

"But I didn't intend getting into that. You know all that. A boy of your intelligence doesn't have to be told what this game is all about."

"Thank you," I said.

"No boy of mine has ever broken the same rule twice."

"Yes sir."

"No boy in all my years of coaching has ever placed his personal welfare above the welfare of the aggregate unit."

"Yes sir."

"Our inner life is falling apart. We're losing control of things. We need more self-sacrifice, more discipline. Our inner life is crumbling. We need to renounce everything that turns us from the knowledge of ourselves. We're getting too far away from our own beginnings. We're roaming all over the landscape. We need to build ourselves up mentally and spiritually. Do that and the body takes care of itself. I learned this as a small boy. I was very sickly, a very sickly child. I had this and that disease. I was badly nourished. My legs were no thicker than the legs of that chair. But I built myself up by determination and sacrifice. The mind first and then the body. It was a lonely life for a boy. I had no friends. I lived in an inner world of determination and silence. Mental resolve. It made me strong; it prepared me. Things return to their beginnings. It's been a long circle from there to here. But all the lessons hold true. The inner life must be disciplined just as the hand or eye. Loneliness is strength. The Sioux purified themselves by fasting and solitude. Four days without food in a sweat lodge. Before you went out to lament for your nation, you had to purify yourself. Fasting and solitude. If you can survive loneliness, you've got an inner strength that can take you anywhere. Four days. You wore just a bison robe. I don't think there's anything makes more sense than self-denial. It's the only way to attain moral perfection. I've wandered here and there. I've made this and that mistake. But now I'm back and I'm back for good. A brave nation needs discipline. Purify the will. Learn humility. Restrict the sense life. Pain is part of the harmony of the nervous system."

I said nothing.

"What I called you in here for," Creed said.

"Yes sir."

"Do you know the reason?"

"Why I'm here? I assume because I walked off the field."

"I knew that exploit was coming," he said. "In one form or another it had to come. It was just a matter of time. I knew about Penn State and Syracuse. Sooner or later you had to make a gesture. Do something. Upset things. Test yourself—yourself more than me. I've been waiting. Every team I've ever coached had at least one boy who had to make the gesture. I've been waiting all season. You did it at other schools in one form or another and I knew you'd do it here. It's off your chest now. You can settle down. What I called you in here for. Kimbrough graduates in the spring. You're offensive captain."

"I never expected anything like this," I said. "I'm not a senior. Doesn't it go to seniors?"

"Never mind that."

"Frankly I thought I was here to be disciplined."

"Maybe that's what it all amounts to. I'll be demanding extra. I'll be after you every minute. As team leader you'll be setting an example for the rest of them. You'll have to give it everything you've got and then some."

"I'll be ready," I said.

"I know you will, son. You'll find Oscar Veech in the training room. Send him in here."

"One thing I've been meaning to ask since the minute I walked in. What's that picture taped to the wall? Who is that in the picture? Is it anybody in particular?"

"Somebody sent that picture to me many years ago. Looks like it came from some kind of religious book for kids. People were always sending me things. Good luck things or prayers or all kinds of advice. Not so much now. They've been keeping pretty quiet of late. But that's a Catholic saint. I've kept that picture with me for many years now. Teresa of Ávila. She was a remarkable woman. A saint of the church. Do you know what she used to do in order to remind herself of final things?"

"Something to do with a skull, I think."

"She used to eat food out of a human skull."

"I'll go find Veech," I said.

In my room later I became depressed. No American accepts the deputy's badge without misgivings; centuries of heroic lawlessness have captured our blood. I felt responsible for a vague betrayal of some local code or lore. I was now part of the apparatus. No longer did I circle and watch, content enough to be outside the center and even sufficiently cunning to plan a minor raid or two. Now I was the law's small tin glitter. Suck in that gut, I thought.

Jimmy Fife came in and sat on Anatole's bed. Fife was a defensive back who had been disabled all year, a ruptured spleen. Someone had accidentally kicked him during a practice session the previous spring. He had been very close to death. Many players still kidded him about it.

"Nix went wild last night and started throwing ash cans through windows. His ass has likely had it."

"Coach made me captain," I said. "As of now, I captain the offense."

"Congrats," Fife said.

"I don't know if it's good or bad. I feel a little bit upset. I guess I just have to get used to it. So Nix went berserk."

"Completely amuck," he said. "I saw the last part of it. It took six people to carry him off. It was a real fist-swinging melee. I didn't get anywhere near it. Stupid to expose the spleen to contact at this point."

"But Nix was out in the snow with us a little while ago. I just realized. I'm sure Nix was there. He was in the game we were playing out in the blizzard."

"I don't doubt it," Fife said. "He's an animal. He's an animal's animal. The animals themselves would vote him all-animal. After a night like last night anybody else would be in bed for a week. Animalism aside, I'll tell you what he really is. He's a nihilist. He himself says so. I've had conversations with the guy. He blames it on his name. Nix meaning no, no thanks, nothing."

"I've never talked to the guy," I said.

"I've had conversations with the guy. He's pretty interesting, albeit a little bit stereo."

"What do you mean—stereo?"

"I mean psycho. Did I say stereo? What a funny word to use."

"You said albeit a little bit stereo."

"Did I say albeit? That's incredible, Gary. I'd never use a word like that. A word like that is way out of my province."

"But you used it, Jimmy. I'm certain."

"I must have been speaking in tongues," Fife said.

He bounced on the bed a few times, his mouth wide open, and I thought he might be trying to cast out a minor playful word-demon.

"Anyway," I said, "Nix has probably had it."

"Sure, they'll get him for the windows. It's my guess he'll be gone for good. Have you heard about Conway's insects?"

"Offensive captain," I said. "That means I go out for the coin toss. If Coach doesn't object I think I'll go out with my helmet off. I'll carry it rather than wear it. I think it looks better. It sort of humanizes the coin toss. Then I can put it on again as I come running off."

"Who's the new defensive captain?" Fife said.

"I don't know. Coach didn't say and I didn't ask."

"How is he? I hear he's the same."

"He's in a wheelchair," I said.

"A wheelchair."

"Don't ask me why. Something to do with his legs, I guess. At least that's what he seemed to intimate. Maybe not."

"Where's Bloomers?"

"I don't know."

"John Butler tells me he's been hearing strange noises at night. These noises come from the other side of Butler's wall. The other side of Butler's wall is right here. It goes on for hours. Butler says it goes *teek teek teek teek*."

"I don't know anything about it."

"Conway," he said. "I started to tell you about Conway's insects. He's got this tremendous assortment of insects in his room. A few days ago he went out in the desert and dug them out of hibernation and brought them back to his room. Everybody's been going in there to look at them. I think he wants to put them in some kind of cage or giant bowl. Arrange it like their natural surroundings. Some dirt, some small plants, some rocks. And then see what happens."

"It sounds horrible."

"I think it might be interesting, Gary. We'll get a chance to see what happens."

"What could happen?"

"They could reproduce. They could fight among themselves. I don't know. But it might be interesting. Conway knows all about insects. They're his field. He was telling us all about it. It's pretty interesting from a number of viewpoints."

"Has he built this thing he's going to build yet?"

"Work on that starts tomorrow. For the time being he's keeping them in a number of jars."

"What kind of number? How many insects are there?"

"Maybe forty all told. All different kinds. Beetles, spiders, scorpions—mostly beetles. The spider incidentally is not an insect. The spider is an arachnid. Let's go take a look."

"I'd just as soon stay here, I think, Jimmy."

"A quick look," he said.

"How quick?"

"In and out, Gary."

"I've got things to do. We'd have to make it a very quick look."

"We'll just stick our heads in the door. Wap. In and out."

We went down the hall. I saw two people come out of Conway's room. Four others were there when we walked in. Conway escorted us around the room. There were ten or eleven large jars. Most of the insects seemed to be asleep.

"Tell Gary about the tiger beetle," Fife said.

"The tiger beetle is a very interesting creature. The tiger beetle hunts by night. It moves swiftly over the ground or it climbs trees. It goes after caterpillars mostly."

"What's so interesting about that?" I said.

"Tell him about the radioactivity."

"Insects are highly resistant to radioactivity," Conway said. "In case of an all-out something-or-other, they'll probably end up taking over the planet. All the birds will be killed off by the fallout. But the insect resists fallout. He won't have birds feeding off him. He'll be able to reproduce freely."

"Most people are aware of that," I said.

"But I'll tell you a mistake almost everybody makes. It concerns the spider. The spider is not an insect. The spider is an arachnid."

"I know that. Almost everybody knows that."

"He doesn't know about the wolf spider," Fife said. "Tell him about the wolf spider and the little spiderlings. How they ride on her back."

"The wolf spider has eight eyes. It spins no web. When the female's eggs hatch, the little spiderlings ride on her back for about a week."

"The scavenger beetle," Fife said. "Tell him about the scavenger. I like the part where it lays the eggs."

"The scavenger beetle is equipped with a set of digging claws. It can bury a dead mouse or a dead bird in two or three hours. Something many times its own size. The beetle then lays eggs on the dead carcass. These eggs hatch very quickly and the larvae come out and start eating the meat of the dead bird. The scarab beetle is of the scavenger type. It lives on dung. The scarab had been a symbol of immortality since the ancient Egyptians."

Dennis Smee walked in.

"Somebody told me to ask you about radioactivity."

"Insects are highly resistant to radioactivity," Conway said. "Man dies if he's exposed to six hundred units. Mr. Insect can survive one hundred thousand units and more. And he won't have birds feeding off him. He'll be able to reproduce freely. There won't be any balance in the sense we know it."

"Balance," Fife said. "The equality of effective values with respect to the applied number of reduced symbolic quantities on each side of an equation, excluding combined derivatives."

Terry Madden came in and congratulated me on my co-captaincy. Everybody shook my hand and wished me well. Then Lee Roy Tyler and Ron Steeples came in to look at the insects. Steeples was wearing a red golf glove on his right hand.

"Where you going, Gary?" he said.

"Things to do."

In my room I wrote a long hysterical letter on the subject of space-time. Even though I knew nothing about space-time, the letter was fairly easy to write. It practically wrote itself. When I was finished I tried to decide to whom it had been written. This itself seemed the most important thing about the letter. To whom was it going? Whose name would sail, unsuspecting, on that extended text? (Whichever name, it would be minus the word *Dear* and followed by a dour colon—overly formal perhaps but more unfeigned than the mock-casual comma.) I thought of a dozen people and concluded that none was worthy. I left the six pieces of paper on the old brown saddle blanket atop Anatole's bed. Bing Jackmin walked in and took a chair.

"Did you hear?" he said.

"What?"

"He's wearing those sunglasses again. Shaved skull and dark glasses. What the hell does it mean?"

"I don't know," I said. "It probably doesn't mean anything. He's a remote individual. The dark glasses conceal him. Or conceal whatever's around him. I don't know."

"What about the skull, Gary?"

"I don't know why he shaved. I have no idea."

"Don't you care to speculate?"

"I leave that to the joint chiefs. I'm just a lowly captain."

"I heard, Gary. Nice going. Although you'll probably regret it as soon as Coach starts in with the tongue-lashings. He saves that stuff for the quarterback and the two captains."

"I know," I said. "He told me to expect trouble."

"Verbal tongue-lashings. Public humiliation."

"I know, Bing."

"First time it happens you'll wish you never even saw a football. You'll experience total personality destructuring."

"We're wasting space-time," I said. "I have a lot to do."

"I'll tell you why I came in here in the first place. I want to grow a beard. I want hair. It's a question of increasing my personal reality. I'm serious about this, Gary."

"What color beard?"

"Gary, I'm serious now."

"Because if you want it the same color as the hair on your head, you'll have a lot easier time growing it."

"I'd like you to talk to Coach. You're one of the captains now. You've got a power base. There's no word out on excess hair. I want you to find out what the word is."

"It's very curious," I said. "All these juxtapositions of hair and non-hair. I half expect Anatole to come walking in with a long white mane down over his shoulders."

"Talk to Coach. Talk to him. It's just an ounce of hair but it'll mean a whole lot to me. I'm becoming too psychomythical in my orientation. I need a reality increment. Find out what the word is."

"He'll ignore me, Bing. He'll just look away in disgust."

"Keep after him. Hound the son of a bitch. I want some excess hair. I'm serious about this. Tell him I'm willing to shave it off when spring practice begins. But I need a beard now. Try to explain personalized reality to him."

"These are subglacial matters," I said. "I can't just snap my fingers and decide. Besides I have no real power. He'll just look away in disgust. All I can do for the moment is think about it. I'll think about it."

"Think about it," Bing said. "I'll be in Conway's room looking at the insects."

I went for a walk. It had stopped snowing. The lamps were lit along the straight white paths. It was dinnertime and everyone was inside. I inhaled deeply, feeling the air enter and bite. My right shoulder ached from the game in the snow. I rotated my arm slowly. Then I saw Alan Zapalac coming down the library steps, an enormous yellow scarf circling his neck two or three times and terminating at his kneecap. He made his way carefully, using the heel of his right shoe to probe each step for ice beneath the stacked snow. I waited for him at the foot of the stairs. He wore an armband on which was printed the word TREES, green on light blue.

"Escort me to the administration building," he said. "If I fall down and break my leg, I'll need somebody to tell the others not to move me. If you weren't here and if it happened, breaking my leg, they'd come along and move me, broken bone and all. If you yourself slip, which I doubt will happen with your athletic prowess and tremendous genetic advantages, make sure you don't reach out and grab for me. I know that's everybody's natural instinct but I want you to fight off the urge because if you take me with you with my delicate bone structure I'm as good as dead. They'd probably use me in one of their experiments with hogs or chickens. None of my organs would be safe. Tomorrow you'd go behind that white building that looks like somebody pinned a surgical gown over it and in that pen they've got out back for the inoculated animals you'd see a hog walking along with my kidneys inside it, urinating the last dregs of my life into the alfalfa."

"I'm going that way anyway," I said.

"Good, good, good. How's the lady friend?"

"Myna," I said. "Myna's fine as far as I know."

"I'm no good at names. My students are catching on. In one of my classes there's an all-out hoax being perpetrated, supposedly at my expense. They've invented a student. His name is Robert Reynolds. After class somebody always comes up to my desk to ask a question. Whoever it is, he makes it a point to identify himself by name. It's a different boy every day but the name is always Robert Reynolds. I get test papers from Robert Reynolds. Yesterday there was a new attendance card in my bunch, very authentic looking, full of IBM holes. It was Robert Reynolds' card. So I called out his name when I took the attendance. Naturally somebody answered. Everybody else said *here*. But the Robert Reynolds person said *present*. You could sense the laughter being contained, the greatness of their mission, how they had banded together to perpetrate this thing at my expense, the teacher, the so-called font of wisdom. For the moment I'm playing dumb. I'm letting them get away with it. They think I don't know what's going on. But there are ploys and there are counterploys. Getting back for a second. Your lady friend. Why is she so fat?"

"The responsibilities of beauty," I said. "She thinks they'd be too much for her. They'd cause her to change. I think I tend to agree."

"My wife-to-be is a white Protestant fencepost. A very one-dimensional body-shape. She's rough and tough, a classic Midwest bitch. When we argue she squeezes the flesh on the back of my hand. She really twists it hard, pinching it simultaneously. Her ~~face becomes very~~ Protestant ~~if you know what~~ I mean. A Zurich theologian lives inside her."

"I don't understand why you'd want to marry somebody like that. If somebody like that twisted my flesh, to be perfectly frank with you I think I'd hit her. I'd hate to have my flesh pinched and squeezed on any kind of recurring basis."

"I've never punched or slapped a woman," he said. "I like to body-check them instead, like a hockey player. I smash them into the boards. It surprises them. A body-check is something they can't interpret with their normal uncanniness of knowing exactly how to retaliate, with whatever exact give-and-take, the way only women can do, giving back tenfold but with a genius that makes it seem even steven."

"But why would you marry somebody like that?"

"She loves me. I'm the only person she's ever loved. Sometimes I think I'm the only person in the whole world she's capable of loving. She calls me long-distance every other day. I jump with joy every time the telephone rings. She's three inches taller than I am but why quibble over inches when you're involved in matters of eternal import. Speaking of tall and short, notice the length of my scarf. Little men like to wear long scarfs. The reason for this is lost in the mists of time. But to return to love. ~~Love~~ is a way of ~~salvation. It~~ makes us less imperfect and draws us closer to immortality. I want to stir up ecstasy in my soul. I want to ascend ~~to the world of~~ forms. Love basically is the suspension of gravity. It's an ascent to higher places. The very existence of her love will stir me to deep ecstasy. I'll begin to climb. Notice the selfish element in my scheme."

"You mentioned salvation," I said. "What kind of salvation?"

"I believe in the remission of sins," Zapalac said. "The world's, the nation's, the individual's sins. Do penance and they shall be forgiven. Salvation consists in the remission of sins. Whatever penances can be performed. Whatever denials or offerings up."

"Are you serious?"

"The nation's sins," he said.

"That was the administration building."

"I'm going in the back way. It's part of my overall schemata. I like to turn up behind people's backs. Suddenly there I am, at their shoulder blades, ready to be a friend to the enemies of injustice."

I walked back to Staley Hall. In the dining room I saw Bloomberg sitting with Spurgeon Cole. I put some corn flakes on a tray and joined them.

"How's Coach?" Spurgeon said.

"He's progressing as anticipated."

"I have a feeling," Bloomberg said, "that's he's about ready to shuffle off these mortal coils, as they say in show business."

"How does it feel being captain, Gary?"

"I get to go out for the coin toss. I've always wanted to be part of that. It's tremendously ceremonial without being too pompous."

"He's wearing the dark glasses again," Spurgeon said. "He hasn't worn them in months. Now he's wearing them."

"I know all about it. I have no comment."

"It must mean something, Gary. Dark glasses indoors in the dead of winter."

"It doesn't mean anything. Look at Steeples. Steeples is going around with a gold glove on his hand. What the hell does that mean?"

"Steeples has some kind of infection. It's ugly as hell apparently. He was exposed to something. It's a sort of burn plus a sort of infection. He just wants to keep it hidden."

"Is that all you're eating?" Bloomberg said to me.

"It contains vitamin B, iron and niacin."

"I'm up to three-o-six," he said. "The new mind expands ~~with the~~ old ~~body. I feel more alert~~ every day. I feel revitalized."

Bing Jackmin came over and sat down. His tray held baked ham, mashed potatoes, salad and pound cake. He was looking at me intensely.

"Did you talk to Coach?"

"Give me time," I said.

"There is no time."

"Can't you start growing it and then either keep it going or terminate it when I find out what the word is?"

"Terminate what?" Spurgeon said.

"His excess hair. He wants a beard. Does anybody know what the prevailing attitude is on excess hair?"

"Excess hair is acceptable if it doesn't exceed accepted standards," Spurgeon said.

"There's your answer, Bing."

"I am interested in certain aspects of global violence," Bloomberg said.

"Pass the salt," Bing said.

"This meat," Spurgeon said. "There's something wrong with this meat."

Bloomberg cleared his throat.

"I am an anguished physicist. I take long walks in the country. From time to time I have second thoughts about the super-megaroach aerosol bomb which can kill anything that moves on the whole earth in a fraction of a microsecond and which I alone invented and marketed. As I walk the peaceful country lanes of the Institute for Abstract Speculation and Sneak Attacks way out there in an unmarked site somewhere in the Pacific Northeast, a television crew films my every step. The director asks me to gaze up over the treetops and to squint slightly into the late afternoon sun. At such moments I think of my roach-bomb and I am filled with a sense of deep humility and also with a feeling of fantastic bloodsucking power. And I am reminded of the comforting words of the famed celestial song of the Hindus. *What is this crime I am planning, O Krishna?* So you see, my friends, I am not without a sense of history nor of personal responsibility. I have a human side and I love the classics. As I smoke my pipe and play a quiet game of chess with my lovely wife, the mother of three fine boys by a previous marriage, I like to ruminate on the nature of man. What brought us forth from the primordial slime? Whither are we headed? What is the grand design? And pondering these vast questions over cheese and port, I come to the realization that one terminal bomb more or less makes small difference in this ever-expanding universe of ours."

"Would somebody please pass the salt," Bing said.

"I am interested in the violent man and the ascetic. I am on the verge of concluding that an individual's capacity for violence is closely linked with his ascetic tendencies. We are about to rediscover that austerity is our true mode. In our future meditations we may decide to seek the devil's death. In our silence and terror we may steer our technology toward the metaphysical, toward the creation of some unimaginable weapon able to pierce spiritual barriers, to maim or kill whatever dark presence envelops the world. You will say this seems an unlikely matter to engage the talents of superrational man. But it is precisely this kind of man who has been confronting the unreal, the paradoxical, the ironic, the satanic. After all, the ultimate genius of modern weapons, from the purely theoretical standpoint, is that they destroy the living. We can go on from there to frame any number of provocative remarks but we will resist the temptation. We all know that life, happiness, fulfillment come surging out of particular forms of destructiveness. The moral system is enriched by violence put to positive use. But as the capacity for violence grows in the world, the regenerative effects of specific violent episodes become less significant. The capacity overwhelms everything. The mere potential of one form of violence eclipses the actuality of other forms. I am interested in these things. I am also interested in the discontinuation of contractions. Medial letters are as valid as any others. I have already begun to revise my speech patterns accordingly."

We were all laughing, not knowing exactly why. Maybe we thought Bloomberg was crazy. Or maybe we laughed because it was the only reaction we could trust, the only one that could keep us at a safe distance. Anatole, replying to the laughter, tapped his spoon against the plastic tray to his right. I finished my corn flakes and proceeded, as arranged, to the library.

Myna was sitting alone in one of the rooms downstairs. Her table was covered with books, all abandoned there, many left open (a breach in their solemnity), massive volumes in tiny lines of print. Beyond the table were long high stacks, reeking a bit of perspiration (presumably human), the 900 series, history in its smelliest caparisons, each dark aisle booby-trapped with a metal stool or two. It was fairly pleasant to be there, the library as womb, fluorescent refuge from chaos or rain. Myna was reading Zap Comix. I sat next to her, then reached across the table and pulled a book toward me. It was a dictionary, opened to facing pages that began with *Kaaba* and ended with *kef*. Myna looked different somehow. I hadn't seen her in about a week and it took me a couple of seconds to realize that her face was much more clear, almost completely blotchless. She leaned toward the dictionary. We read the definitions to each other for a while. Some of them were extremely funny. Then we selected certain words to read aloud. We read them slowly, syllable by syllable, taking turns, using at times foreign or regional accents, then replaying the sounds, perhaps backward, perhaps starting with a middle syllable, and finally reading the word as word, overpronouncing slightly, noses to the page as if in search of protomorphic spoor. Some of the words put Myna into a state of mild delirium; she thought their beauty almost excessive. We kept reading for half an hour. The words were ways of touching and made us want to speak with hands. We went into a far corner of the high stacks. There I started taking off her dress. The great cumulus breasts came rolling out of hand-beaded blue Victorian velvet. We laughed loudly, then tried to quiet each other with soft punches to the arm. A button fell to the floor, rolling unsteadily into a distant corner. I made bubbling noises, rubbing my face in her breasts, scratching an itch just under my eye with her left nipple. Together we got the dress down over her hips, hitting each other lightly to warn the laughter off, and in time it was at her feet. I made strange noises of anticipation (*gwa, gwa*) and this made her hit me with both hands, but weakly because of the laughter rocking inside her. We heard something at the doorway and made faces at each other, exaggerated fright-masks, and I looked past her and through the slightly tilted rows of books, tilts and counter-tilts, angles commenting on other angles, centuries misplaced by slumbering hands, the entire self-contradictory mass looming humorously over my darling's epic breasts. There was no one in the doorway. I plucked a chord or two on the tense elastic of her iridescent panties. Sign of tiny pink ridges, wave-shaped, about her buoyant waist. We kissed and bit. She tickled certain vulnerable areas below my ribs. We touched, patted and licked. It may be impossible to explain why it seemed so very important to get her completely naked. Our hands rolled the pants past her hips and thighs. To mark the event I brought new noises to the room, vowel sounds predominating. Myna stepped away from the clothes, aware of the moment's dynamics, positing herself as the knowable word, the fleshmade sigh and syllable. She was beautiful, broad as a many-sectioned cubistic bather, conceptually new, cloud-bosomed, ultimate. To be forever loved in ways unworthy. In seconds we would be ingathered, amassment of hair and limbs, unbrokenly focused, hunting each other in the melting cave. Some one or thing at the doorway's edge. No: closer. A woman lurking in the stacks. I could see her, four rows away, shoulder to nose between the shelves. I gestured to Myna of the danger nearby. Then I tried to help her get into her clothes, accidentally bumping her once with my knee so that she fell forward over a stool. We looked at each other, not knowing whether to be alarmed by the approaching footsteps, or amused, or merely indifferent. I directed her toward a small alcove in which was placed a bust of some unnamed immortal. Then I opened a book and began to read in a soft voice a number of reflections on an ancient war I had never even heard of until that moment. The woman was Mrs. Berry Trout, an administrator of some kind. She gave me an unloving look.

"What's your name, young man?"

"Robert Reynolds," I said, slipping into my southern accent.

29

ONE NIGHT THE MAJOR and I played a crude form of war game in his motel room. He sat facing me, about four feet away, a small table between us. On the table were pencils, pads, maps, and a chart that I was having a great deal of trouble trying to read upside down. The major said that one of the big problems with war games, whether they were being played at the Pentagon, at NORAD or Fort Belvoir, at a university or think tank, was the obvious awareness on the part of all participants that this wasn't the real thing. (What we were playing, he added, was barely the simulated thing; we had no computer, intelligence reports, projection screens, and only a few numerical estimates of troop units, missile inventories, production capacities.) The gaming environment, as he called it, could never elicit the kind of emotions generated in times of actual stress; therefore gaming was probably just a second-rate guide (hopefully not too misleading) to what might be expected from governments when the armies were poised and lithe missiles were rising from their silos. As I sat there, listening, I wondered why we were meeting in a motel. It seemed to me that the major's house should have been ready for occupancy by this time and that his family should have joined him. However, it did not seem appropriate to comment.

He looked through the material in front of him, then glanced around the room before spotting what he wanted, a world atlas. It was on the bed, about eight feet away. He asked me to get it for him.

"Now this scenario is premised on futuribles," he said. "The basic situation as I've set it up for us is definitely in the area of what we know to be projected crisis situations. It could happen. Tensions. Possible accidents. Unrelated hostilities. Or maybe not so unrelated. Precedents: one act of aggression tending to legalize another. Then finally a showdown between two major powers. That's the basic situation, the starting point or premise as I'll conceptualize it for you in a minute. What happens after that is up to us. Now, before I forget, the two major powers are just who you might expect them to be except I've changed their names slightly, just to make them a little less appealing or distasteful to our emotions, as the case may be. COMRUS is one and AMAC is the other. It's not supposed to fool anybody and it just gives you a glimpse of what we might be able to do in the future in terms of totally our own situations, not depending on existing bodies or preconceptions. So it's just to neutralize our emotions a little bit. In fact I haven't bothered to change much else, just a designation here and there since I'm just beginning to get into this. So we're a little bit disorganized and inconsistent this first time and we'll probably have to improvise as we go along. But to get back, what happens after I introduce this thing is up to us. We might become wildly implausible or we might run right through the crisis game from escalation to escalation with absolutely traditional military logic—if there is such a thing and I'm not sure there is. We might not even get to the point of using nuclear weapons. Or we might start pitching right off."

The major outlined the crisis.

It begins in the Sea of Japan. An AMAC destroyer of the Seventh Fleet, on maneuvers, is strafed by two NORKOR MIGs. Damage is light; there are no casualties. Two days later a Polaris submarine in the East Siberian Sea is reported missing. In Germany three high-ranking agents defect to the West; unmarked planes drop leaflets over East Berlin, over Prague, over Budapest. There are a dozen explosions of suspicious origin at military bases throughout Spain and Turkey. An unmanned AMAC intelligence plane is downed by COMCHIN missiles in the Formosa Strait. Fires break out on successive days at the atomic power laboratory in Los Alamos and in the civil defense command center at Cheyenne Mountain. The commander of an AMAC truck convoy, following orders, fails to stop at an East German roadblock along the Autobahn; shots are exchanged and the convoy breaks through. A Dutch-built factory ship, being delivered to NORKOR, is struck by torpedoes and sunk outside Chongjin. COMRUS objects strongly. Several explosions damage Nike-Hercules installations on Okinawa. COMCHIN negotiators suspend talks with the Japanese over ownership of the Senkaku Islands in the East China Sea. Within a time-frame of ten hours there are over a dozen small clashes, involving demonstrators and troops, on both sides of the Berlin wall. Messages are exchanged. There are reports that Egyptian troops have retaken El Arish. COMRUS demands gradual allied withdrawal from West Berlin. COMRUS demands withdrawal of all AMAC auditors in Indochina. NATO reports large-scale troop movements west of Leipzig, east of Lübeck, near Klatovy. COMRUS claims an overkill factor of three in relation to Western Europe. A dozen light bombers of the Warsaw Pact air forces are spotted over Bonn. An RAF recon-

naissance plane is shot down by MIG–23s after violating
East German airspace. More ultimatums. Troops of the
Warsaw Pact nations, using conventional weapons, clash
with NATO forces at three different locales along the
West German frontier. SAC is put on alert. Twelve
COMRUS infantry divisions—about a hundred twenty
thousand men—are moved to Western Europe from Lake
Baikal north of Mongolia. AMAC navy jets from the
carrier *Kitty Hawk* engage COMRUS aircraft two hundred
miles south of Vladivostok. COMCHIN explodes a thirty-
megaton device at its test site in northern Tibet. The use
of tactical nuclear weapons by an AMAC ground unit in
West Germany is at first denied and then claimed to be
accidental. A brief cessation of hostilities. Charges and
countercharges. COMRUS (Staley) and AMAC (Harkness) are approaching a state of war.

The major went through this scenario very slowly. He
referred to his maps at least ten times, showing me the
precise locations of certain countries, cities, military
bases. Often he paused during these map readings as if
waiting for me to comment, perhaps on the subtle geographic patterns he had devised for the various conflicts. I
had trouble finding any particular pattern but I could tell
quite easily how much time and work he had put into
the project. It seemed almost sad. I was hardly a compe-
tent enemy. I had no experience in this sort of thing. I
had been plagued by joyous visions of apocalypse but I
was not at all familiar with the professional manipula-
tions, both diplomatic and military, which might normally
precede any kind of large-scale destruction. All I could
do was try to react intelligently, if that word can be used,
to whatever the major did with his divisions, his air force,
his warships, his missiles. I wasn't feeling very involved. In
fact I considered the scenario somewhat boring despite
all the frenzy and tension. At this point the major set
down the rules for the second and final part of the game,
the part in which I would participate, and he also invited
me to share an elaborate chart he had prepared, using

information taken from a study by some military research institute. Before we started, he said he was working on a totally simulated world situation—seven major nations of his own making, seventeen major cities, an unspecified (secret) number of military installations, fairly complete demographic, economic, social, religious, racial and meteorological characteristics for each nation. He would have it ready for us in two or three weeks; it would be a much more pure form of gaming than the one we were using now.

At length we began. It took only twelve major steps or moves to complete the game and yet we were at it for more than three hours. It was the strangest thing I had ever taken part in. There were insights, moves, minor revelations that we savored together. Silences between moves were extremely grave. Talk was brief and pointed. Small personal victories (of tactics, of imagination) were genuinely satisfying. Mythic images raged in my mind.

(1) Nuclear-powered COMRUS submarines enter the Gulf of Mexico. An AMAC carrier of the Sixth Fleet is badly damaged by enemy aircraft in the Mediterranean.

(2) Seven COMRUS trawlers are sunk off the coast of Oregon. Missiles fired by Vulcan surface-to-air batteries destroy two MIG–21 fighter planes near Mannheim.

(3) COMRUS troops invade Western Europe. The atomic test site at Amchitka in the Aleutians is believed wiped out.

(4) SAC bombers assume maximum attack posture. The President leaves the White House situation room and boards Air Force One.

(5) COMRUS explodes a one-megaton nuclear device high in the air over territory west of Brussels, causing virtually no damage to property.

(6) SAC bombers attack a limited number of COMRUS military targets, using low-yield kiloton bombs to reduce collateral damage.

(7) Partial evacuation of major COMRUS cities. ICBMs hit strategic targets throughout Europe. COMRUS

medium-range bombers attack AMAC air bases in England. Long-range missiles hit Grand Forks AFB in North Dakota.

(8) AMAC ICBMs, B–52s and B–58s strike at air bases, dams, bridges, railroads and missile sites deep inside COMRUS territory. The Tallinn missile defense system is hit and partially destroyed. The antimissile complexes on the western outskirts of Moscow are badly damaged. AMAC orders almost total evacuation of major cities.

(9) COMRUS orders almost total evacuation of major cities. Three Polaris submarines in the North Atlantic are destroyed. Radar installations in Alaska and Greenland are wiped out. Titan installations surrounding Tucson in Arizona are hit by COMRUS SS–9 missiles with warheads totaling nearly 100 megatons. Tucson is rendered uninhabitable by fallout.

(10) The city-busting begins. Selected population centers within COMRUS borders are hit by Minuteman 3 ICBMs carrying MIRV warheads. Polaris submarines in the North Sea and the Baltic fire missiles at selected sites. SAC bombers raid selected cities from Murmansk to Vladivostok.

(11) Washington, D.C., is hit with a 25-megaton device. New York and Los Angeles are hit with SS–11 missiles.

(12) SIMcap dictates spasm response.

The telephone rang. Major Staley turned quickly in his chair, terrified for a long second, and then simply stared at the commonplace black instrument as it continued to ring.

30

Myna returned from Christmas vacation many pounds lighter. When I saw her, I didn't know how to react. She was having coffee with the Chalk sisters in the student lounge and I stood in the doorway a moment, trying to prepare a suitable remark or two. She was wearing a white cotton blouse; her hair was combed straight back and ribboned at the nape of the neck. Vera Chalk saw me and waved me over, gesturing urgently, her face expressing news of colossal wonders. The sisters put their hands on me as soon as I sat down, scratching at my arms and chest in their glee at finding an object toward which to direct their effusions.

"Look at her, Gary."

"I'm looking. Hi. I'm virtually speechless."

"Hi," Myna said.

"It's just the beginning," Esther said. "She's got twenty more pounds to go. She's lost twenty and she's got twenty to go. In other words she's halfway there."

"Just look at her," Vera said. "She's like a new person. She looks unbelievable. I'm so happy for her. I can't believe how much better she looks. Gary, what do you think?"

"I think it's unbelievable."

"I'm ecstatic on her behalf. I really am."

"Don't use that word," Esther said.

"Ecstatic."

"You know how much I hate that word, you spiteful bitch."

"Ec-stat-ic."

"Now quit it, Vera."

"You're not supposed to call me that. Gary, she knows how much I loathe and despise my name."

"Vera."

"Ecstatic. More ecstatic. Most ecstatic."

"Vera beera. One little lira for a glass of Vera beera."

"Ecstasy of ecstasies."

"Enough," I said.

"I'll stop if she will," Esther said. "Besides we're supposed to be discussing Myna. Gary, don't you think it's unbelievable?"

"It's unbelievable. It really is."

"Are you just saying that? Or do you really think it?"

"I'm just saying it. I don't know what to think. It's too early yet. I need time to reflect."

"Don't be such a picayune shit," Vera said.

"I had to do it, Gary. It became a question of self-definition. I was just moping along like an unreal person. I used to look forward to nothing-type things. I never really faced my own reality. I was satisfied just consuming everything that came along. But after only twenty pounds, things are already starting to be different. I'm beginning to catch my own reflection everywhere I go. I'm being forced to face myself as a person instead of somebody who just mopes along consuming everything that's put in front of her. Gary, I've spent too much time on nothing-type things. I used to think three meals ahead. I used to be satisfied figuring out which dress I was going to wear with whichever dumb shoes. I used to work these things out in my head for hours. It really made me happy working out my combinations. These shoes, that dress, this bracelet. The sweater with the purple star and the dumb blue boots. The sculptured brass peace symbol strung on rawhide and the turquoise dishrag tunic with drawstring neck and full sleeves. These things were my doggy treats. I did a good trick and I got a doggy treat.

The whole process took me further away from myself and made my life a whole big thing of consumption, consuming, consume. Purple-star sweaters, antique pendants, beaded chokers, organic nuts, horoscopes, science-fiction movies, four-dollar transparent soap, big English cars, Mexican villas, ecology, pink rolling paper, brownies, seaweed with my pork chops, soy noodles, dacron, rayon, orlon acrylic, Fortrel polyester, Lycra spandex, leather, vinyl, suede, velvet, velours, canvas. I shoveled it all in and all I did was bury my own reality and independentness. The whole business of going to Mexico to do nothing but smoke dope was all part of the fatness thing. Gary, I know you liked me fat but at least with the responsibilities of beauty I'll have a chance to learn exactly or pretty exactly what I can be, with no built-in excuses or cop-outs or anything. I'm not just here to comfort you. You can't expect to just come searching for me for comfort. I want other thing now. I'm ready to find out whether I really exist or whether I'm something that's just been put together as a market for junk mail."

"It's all very existential."

"Don't use words," Esther said. "Either you like her this way or you don't. You can't get out of it with words."

"I have to get used to the new situation. I need time to get accustomed."

"Are you sure that's all it is?" Myna said.

"That's all."

"Are you sure it's not that you're definitely against it? Because if you are, it would be better if you said so now."

"I have to get used to it. Time. That's all. I need time."

"You're really sure, Gary?"

"Myna, we've known each other for a number of months. We've been very close to each other. We've shared some unforgettable moments. Would I lie to you?"

"No, I don't think you would, Gary. Not in a pinch."

"Define pinch."

"He's being picayune again," Esther said. "If he can't see what's staring him in the face, he needs more than time. I think he's being real dippy about this."

"So do I," Vera said.

"He's being ridiculous beyond belief."

"For once I have to agree with you. It's nice to think alike for a change. In fact the situation makes me ecstatic."

"Oh you bitch. You damn rotten bitch."

"Ecstatico."

"And you're the one who's into the gospels. Who's into charity and love thy neighbor. Who comes around yapping to me about the power of miracles."

"Without belief in miracles, we are like reeds shaken with the wind," Vera said.

"She's into miracles real heavy."

"I'm a miracle freak, Gary."

I walked back to Staley Hall. It was a blank afternoon, windless and pale, not too cold, the sun hidden, a faint haze obscuring the reduplicated landscape beyond the campus. I went to my room. Bloomberg was in bed, neatly blanketed, reading one of my ROTC manuals.

"They use simple declarative sentences," he said.

I put my coat away and looked out the window for a while. Then I stared at my right thumb. It seemed important to create every second with infinite care, as at the beginning or nearing the end of momentous ordeals. I spent ten minutes learning a new word. Finally, in my gray corduroy trousers and gray shirt, I went down the hall to Taft Robinson's room.

I paused in his doorway, realizing suddenly that I spent a good deal of time in doorways, that I had always spent a lot of time in doorways, that much of my life had been passed this way. I was forever finding myself pausing in a doorway or standing before a window, looking into rooms and out of them, waiting to be tapped on the shoulder by an impeccably dressed gentleman whose flesh has grown over his mouth.

Taft sat cross-legged on the bed, his back to the wall, a sagging newspaper spread from knee to knee. I took a chair by the door. The room seemed slightly more bare than it had the last time I'd visited. Perhaps there was one less chair now or something gone from the floor, a waste-basket or magazine rack.

Taft wore his dark glasses. We were silent for a time. He looked at the newspaper. I didn't experience any particular sense of tension in the room. Sooner or later one of us would say or do something. Then either or both of us would be in a position to decide exactly what had been said or done. I thought of going to stand by the window so that I might assess more clearly and from a somewhat greater altitude the relevant words or action. Then I realized that the very act of going to stand by the window would be the action itself, the selfsame action subject to interpretation. Taft continued to look at the newspaper. I was getting annoyed at the direction of my thoughts. My eyes attempted to focus upon the room's precise geometric center—that fixed point equidistant from the four corners and midway between ceiling and floor. Then Taft's left shoulder twitched a bit, an involuntary shudder, a minor quake in some gleaming arctic nerve. That faint break in basic structure was enough to alter every level of mood. It was all I could do to keep my lips from inching into a slight smile.

"A hundred thousand welcomes," he said.

"Thought I'd drop by."

"Come right in. Find a chair and make yourself right at home. I see you've already got a chair. If I'm not mistaken, you're already in the room and you're already seated."

"That's correct. I'm here and seated. What you see, in fact, is exactly what you think you see."

"We might as well begin then."

"Begin what?" I said.

"The dialogue. The exchange of words. The phrases and sentences."

"I don't really have anything to say, Taft. I just came by to visit. I like it here. It's a nice room. It appeals to me. I really like it. We don't have to talk unless you want to."

"I wouldn't mind talking. But what's there to talk about?"

"I was thinking the same thing when I came down the hall. That's why I say we don't have to talk unless you want to. Or unless I want to. One of us at any rate."

"I'm not very talkative, Gary. I go whole days without saying a word. Although there are times when I get the urge to babble. No subject in particular. Just babble on. Any kind of talk just to talk. But I don't think this is one of my babbling times. So we may have to work at it. I mean what'll we talk about? If we can get together on what to talk about, I'd be willing to talk."

"So would I," I said.

"Should we think separately about possible subjects for conversation and then report back to each other? Or what? I'm open to suggestion."

"There's always the common ground. There's football. I'm sure there's something in the whole vast spectrum of football that we can discuss for a few minutes to our mutual profit. For instance, I might point out that time is flying right along. In three months, you know what— thwack, thwack, thwack. We'll have the pads on. We'll be hitting. Three months plus a few days."

"Spring practice," he said.

"Boosh, boosh, boosh. Thwack, thwack."

"There's not too much for me to say on the subject of spring practice, Gary."

"Why not?"

"I won't be there. I'm all through with football. I don't want to play football anymore."

"That's impossible. You can't be serious. What do you want to do if you don't want to play football?"

"I want to concentrate on my studies."

"Studies? Concentrate on what studies?"

"There are books in this room," he said. "I go to class every day. I think about things. I study. I read and formulate. There's plenty to concentrate on. I'm instructing myself in certain disciplines."

"Taft, you can always fit it in. I mean it's football we're talking about. Nobody reads and studies all day long. You can easily make time for football. I mean it's not swimming or track or some kind of extracurricular thing we're talking about here. It's football. It's *football,* Taft."

"Great big game," he said. "I'm after small things. Tiny little things. Less of white father watching me run. Prefer to sit still."

He did a curious thing then: untied his shoelaces. I took a moment to scan the walls for tape-remnants. Poster of Wittgenstein, I thought. Maybe that's what he'd had up there, or almost had. Dollar ninety-eight poster of philosopher surrounded by Vienna Circle. Two parts to that man's work. What is written. What is not written. The man himself seemed to favor second part. Perhaps Taft was a student of that part.

"You have to admit that football represents a tremendous opportunity," I said. "There's money at the end of all this. And what money can't buy."

"You mean the crowd."

"The everything," I said. "The sense of living an inner life right up against the external or tangible life. Of living close to your own skin. You know what I mean. Everything. The pattern. The morality."

"Maybe I crave the languid smoky dream," he said, slowly and softly, with barely evident self-directed humor, dressing the words in black satin. "That's living close to yourself too. You talk about bringing the inside close to the outside. I'm talking about taking the whole big outside and dragging it in behind me. What's the word they use in northern parts of Africa for that stuff they smoke? Not that I'm planning any kind of holy weed mysticism. I'm too hard edged for that. But there are rewards in contemplation. A new way of life requires a new language."

"All right then, damn it. Money aside. Metaphysics aside. It becomes a question of pursuing whatever it is you do best. It's a damn shame to waste talent like yours. It almost goes against some tenuous kind of equilibrium or master plan. Some very carefully balanced natural mechanism. I'm serious about that."

"If I don't play football, the bobcat will become extinct in Wyoming."

"You're an athlete, Taft."

"So are you, Gary. But I'm not going to talk you out of quitting if you want to quit."

"As an athlete I have serious lapses. I don't play football as much as drift in and out of cloud banks of action and noise. I'm not a one-hundred-percent-in-the-American-grain football player. I tend to draw back now and again in order to make minor discoveries that have no bearing on anything. I conduct spurious examinations. I bullshit myself."

"Gary, you're a credit to your race."

He looked down at the newspaper. I took this as an indication that we had reached the end of the introductory phase. I went to the window and stretched. A two-part yawn elongated the faint reflection of my face. There was little movement to be seen on the campus. It wasn't quite dark yet. A man (perhaps a woman) stared at me from a window of the nearest building. It disturbed me that I couldn't be sure of the person's sex. It's always interesting to stand by a window and exchange looks with an unknown woman in another building. But in this case I couldn't be sure whether I was looking at a man or woman. Therefore it seemed dangerous to get interested. It was definitely much too delicate a matter to involve myself with at the present time. I went back to the chair and sat down. Hunched forward I studied my shoes. I thought of going down to the equipment room to check out the rumor about new uniforms. According to the rumor, the coaching staff had decided on a few slight design changes for next season's uniform. At this very moment people were probably crowding into Billy Mast's room or Randy King's room to talk about the rumor, to embellish it, to swim and play in it. I could go down to the equipment room, check things out, then rush up to Billy Mast's room with whatever information or misinformation I had managed to gather. Then we could all discuss it for an hour or so. I wondered whether the designation CAPT or CO-CAPT would be included on my uniform below the right shoulder or above the number 44 on my back. I hoped the rumor turned out to be true. At the very least I hoped we'd get new headgear. I didn't like the old helmets much. I'd be satisfied with new headgear and with the designation CO-CAPT above my number.

"Here's the way I have it figured," I said. "I have it figured that you came here because of Creed, because he convinced you that he could make a complete football player out of you. Or more than that. It was more, wasn't it? There was something in Creed that appealed to you. Not appealed to you—hit you, struck you as being important. He conveyed some kind of message that caught you just right, the same message I got, the sense of some awful kind of honesty that might flow back and forth between you. There's something chilling about Creed. He seems always to be close to a horrible discovery about himself. He's one of those men who never stops suffering, am I right, and he takes you in on it. If you're in his presence at all, you're almost sure to perceive that he's in some kind of pain. He allows you to get fairly close to it, not all the way but fairly close. And this is what makes you trust him or at least relate to him if you're even slightly sensitive to the man's reality, to that awful honesty he conveys. Am I right or not?"

"I'd have to put that whole subject in historical perspective," Taft said.

"I'm anxious. I'm eager to hear it."

"When it became known that I was leaving Columbia,

a whole bunch of people started coming around. An aggregation. Just a whole bunch of them. Prospectors. Canny little men. Appraisers. All with wrinkles around their eyes and friendly enough smiles that you could see them put the brakes to. They came from all over. They came from the swamps, from the mountains, from the plains, from the lakes. In ten days I heard every variation on every regional accent you can imagine. And it was football all the way. It was facilities, plant, tradition, pride, status. It was which conference is best. It was intersectional rivalry and postseason games. Those people could talk football for six hours straight, ten hours, one whole complete weekend. All but Creed. Those people were all the same, compilers of digits, body counters. Friendly enough. But all in that area."

"Then Big Bend walked in."

"Creed was too much. He was part Satan, part Saint Francis or somebody. He offered nothing but work and pain. He'd whisper in my ear. He'd literally whisper things in my ear. He'd tell me he knew all the secrets but one—what it was like to be black. We'd teach each other. We'd work and struggle. At times he made it sound like some kind of epic battle, him against me, some kind of gigantomachy, two gods at war. Other times he'd sweet-talk me—but not with prospects of glory. No, he'd tell me about the work, the pain, the sacrifice. What it might make of me. How I needed it. How I secretly wanted it. He was going to work me into the ground. He was going to teach me how to get past my own limits. Mind and body. He stressed that more than once. Mind and body. And it would be all work, pain, fury, sweat. No time for nonessential things. We would deny ourselves. We would get right down to the bottom of it. We would find out how much we could take. We would learn the secrets."

"He sold you on pain and sacrifice," I said. "You have to give the man credit for a novel approach. He knew his quarry. He knew how to get you, Taft. No brothers down here. No sisters. No sporting press to record your magic. No cameras. He got you on pain. He knew just what he was doing. I give the man credit. He got you on self-denial, on being alone, on geography."

"Don't make it sound so unnatural, Gary. This place isn't as bad as all that. There are counterbalances of one kind or another."

"I know," I said. "I'm very aware of that. But tell me how it ended. Did you and Creed teach each other? Did you get down to the bottom of it? Does he know you're through with football?"

"I continue to instruct myself in certain disciplines. So in that sense I'm still working my way down to the bottom of it. Creed knows I'm not playing football anymore. He's known for quite a while. He said he was expecting it. I told him I knew he was. We were in that room of his. He's so inside himself, that man. I don't think he sees any need for mobility. I mean whatever it is, it'll come to him. I think that's the way he sees it. It'll come or it won't. I doubt he cares very much. But I'm feeling better about things now that I'm through with football. It was time to cut it loose. I feel better every day."

"What did you teach each other?"

"That kind of question gets us into areas where it's hard to avoid sounding ridiculous. In short we taught each other nothing. That summarizes it pretty neatly, I think. And now it's almost time to face Mecca."

"You're staying here, I assume. Football or no football. There are so many arguments against this place that I assume you're staying."

"I've got this room fixed up just the way I want it."

"Of course. This room. Absolutely."

"I'm not being evasive, Gary. Or keeping traditional distances. I want you to take me literally. Everything I've said is to be taken literally. I've got this room fixed up just the way I want it. It's a well-proportioned room. It has just the right number of objects. Everything is exactly where it should be. It took me a long time to get it this way. Before I came here, I told Creed there was one condition. I room alone. I had to have that, I told him. I guess everybody thought they kept me separated in the name of racial sensitivity. But that wasn't it at all. It was my idea from the beginning. It was the only demand I ever made of Creed. I room alone."

"Two clocks," I said.

"Only a seeming excess. They correct each other. Between them, a balance is arrived at, a notion of how much space has to be reconstructed. Space meaning difference between disagreeing hands."

"Three gray pencils in an ex-marmalade jar on a small, probably oak desk."

"A certain play of shapes. The words on the old marmalade jar. The fact that pencils diminish with use. Affinity of materials."

"A radio."

"The place where words are recycled. The place where villages are burned. That's my Indochina. I listen only at certain times of day for certain periods of time. When time's up, I bring it into silence. It's almost a ceremony."

"Small mark on wall left by tape."

"I believe in static forms of beauty," he said. "I like to measure off things and then let them remain. I try to create degrees of silence. Things in this room are simple and static. They're measured off carefully. When I change something slightly, everything changes. The change becomes immense. My life in here almost resembles a certain kind of dream. You know the way objects in dreams sometimes acquire massive significance. They resound somehow. It's easy to fear objects in dreams. It gets like that in here at times. I seem to grow smaller at times and the room appears almost to lengthen. The spaces between objects become a little bit frightening. I like the colors in here, the way they never move, never change. The room tone changes though. There's a hum at times. There's a low roar. There's a kind of dumb brute chant. I think the room tone changes at different times of day. Sometimes it's oceanic and there's other times when it's just barely there, a sort of small pulse in an attic. The radio is important in this regard. The kind of silence that follows the playing of the radio is never the same as the silence that precedes it. I use the radio in different ways. It becomes almost a spiritual exercise. Silence, words, silence, silence, silence."

"My roommate wets the bed," I said. "It's a little hard for me to evolve any kind of genuine stasis under the circumstances. Somehow pee is inimical to stasis. Although I wouldn't want to have to prove it phenomenologically, if that's the word I want."

"I can see your difficulty."

"What about books, Taft? How do they enter into the scheme? I have a problem in that regard. I like to read about mass destruction and suffering. I spend a lot of time reading stuff that concerns thermonuclear war and things that pertain to it. Horrible diseases, fires raging in the inner cities, crop failures, genetic chaos, temperatures soaring and dropping, panic, looting, suicides, scorched bodies, arms torn off, millions dead. That kind of thing."

"I like to read about the ovens," Taft said.

"What do you mean, the ovens? Are you serious?"

"Atrocities. I like to read about atrocities. I can't help it. I like to read about the ovens, the showers, the experiments, the teeth, the lampshades, the soap. I've read maybe thirty or forty books on the subject. But I like kids best. Putting the torch to kids and their mamas. Smashing kids in the teeth with your rifle butt. Laying waste to villages full of kids. Firing into ditches full of kids, infants, babies, so forth. That's my particular interest. Atrocities in general with special emphasis on kids."

"I can't bear reading about kids."

"I can't either, Gary."

"The thought of children being tortured and killed."

"It's the worst thing there is. I can't bear it. But I've read maybe eight books on it so far. Thirty or forty on the ovens and eight on the kids. It's horrible. I don't know why I keep reading that stuff."

"There must be something we can do," I said.

"It's getting to be time to turn toward Mecca. The black stone of Abraham sits in that shrine in old Mecca, the name of which I'll have to look up again because I keep forgetting it. Not that it matters. A name's a name. A place could just as easily be another place. Abraham was black. Did you know that? Mary the mother of Jesus was black. Rembrandt and Bach had some Masai blood. It's all in the history books if you look carefully enough. Tolstoy was three-eighths black. Euclid was six-fifths black. Not that it means anything. Not that any of it matters in the least. Lord, I think I'm beginning to babble."

He took off the dark glasses and pinched the bridge of his nose in true weariness. His eyes were shut. He began to laugh quietly into the newspaper between his knees, preparing in his own way for whatever religious act was scheduled to follow.

I went downstairs to see what I could find out about the rumor concerning new uniforms. There was nobody around and no sign of uniforms, new or old. I decided to walk over to Zapalac's office, which was located in a cinder-block structure only a hundred yards away. I didn't bother getting a coat. It wasn't very cold and I took my time walking over there. The building was full of small dark rooms, all unoccupied. The walls of Zapalac's office were covered with posters, printed slogans, various symbols of this or that movement. His scarf was there but he wasn't.

In my room at five o'clock the next morning I drank half a cup of lukewarm water. It was the last of food or drink I would take for many days. High fevers burned a thin straight channel through my brain. In the end they had to carry me to the infirmary and feed me through plastic tubes.

For the Sunday cyclist... for the cross-country tourist... whether you ride for better health, for sport, or for the sheer fun of it,

GET

THE COMPLETE BOOK OF BICYCLING

The First Comprehensive Guide
To All Aspects of Bicycles and Bicycling

JUST A FEW OF THE HUNDREDS OF EXCITING TIPS YOU'LL FIND:

- A simple way to increase your cycling efficiency by 30 to 40%—breeze over hilltops while others are struggling behind.
- 13 special safety tips for youngsters.
- How to read a bicycle's specifications to know if you're getting a superior one or a dud.
- How to know whether to buy a 3-speed to start with, or a 10-speed.
- How to select the right kind of equipment for touring or camping.
- How to minimize danger when cycling in the city.

▼ AT YOUR BOOKSTORE OR MAIL THIS COUPON NOW FOR FREE 30-DAY TRIAL ▼

Tom Ainslie shows you how to pick...

More Winners in Harness Racing

THE FIRST AND ONLY BOOK ON THE PRINCIPLES AND TECHNIQUES OF HANDICAPPING *HARNESS* RACES

Here is just a sampling of the hundreds of professional techniques you'll find in Ainslie's Complete Guide to Harness Racing:

• A five-point plan that enables you to win substantial sums at leading half-mile tracks. • A profit-building exception to the rule that a horse's speed should be judged from its two most recent outings. • A warning if you're relying on "suck-alongs" with misleading form. • A special technique for betting when the track is wet. • How to spot "darkened form" and cash a nice ticket. • A tip to protect you against mediocre horses with high earnings.

AT YOUR BOOKSTORE OR MAIL THIS COUPON NOW FOR FREE 30-DAY TRIAL

C5/1